Dark Wind Blowing

Jackie French

An imprint of HarperCollins*Publishers*

First published in Australia by Harpercollins*Publishers* Pty Limited in 2001
First published in Great Britain by Collins in 2002
Collins is an imprint of HarperCollins*Publishers* Ltd
77-85 Fulham Palace Road, Hammersmith, London W6 8JB

The HarperCollins website address is www.**fire**and**water**.com

1 3 5 7 9 8 6 4 2

Text copyright © Jackie French 2002

ISBN 0 00 714017 7

Jackie French asserts the moral right to be
identified as the author of the work

Printed and bound in England
By Clays Ltd, St Ives plc

CHAPTER 1

FRIDAY, 8.10 A.M.

The day began quietly, a normal day like many others. The kitchen smelt of eggs and burnt crumbs, mixed with the hint of cattle droppings seeping through the back door from the fields behind the house. Mike grabbed his bag from the floor.

'Mike, your breakfast's on the table!'

'Mum, I don't have time!'

'Of course you do. It's only ten past eight.' His mother stuck her head around the laundry door, the iron in her hand. She was still wearing her dressing gown over her blue linen skirt and had on her 'going to the gallery' shoes.

'Mum, no one has cooked breakfasts!'

'Breakfast is the most important meal of the day.' Her head vanished again.

'Sheesh, Mum, I'm not a kid any more.'

'Mike, remember your language.'

'Sheesh isn't swearing!'

'Yes, it is. You know perfectly well what it stands for.'

'Mum, you just don't understand.' Mike stopped. There was no point in telling his mum anything. She never listened, or when she did she always had an answer, the sort of 'I must know best because I'm an adult' answer . . . He slumped at the table instead and began to shovel down the scrambled eggs. One spoonful, two . . .

Eggs, eggs, horrible eggs,
They slide down your mouth
And then feed your legs . . .

There was an art to not eating Mum's breakfasts. If you didn't eat any of it she'd nag you till you did. If you ate only one slice of toast and eggs, she'd stress as well. But if you ate part of both slices, and drank a third of the glass of orange juice, the rest just looked like leftovers on the plate.

'Finished, Mum! See you tonight!'

There was a clang as the ironing board was shoved back in its corner and Mike's mother came out of the laundry, adjusting the collar of her blouse. 'What time will you be home?'

'Dunno. Might go round to Budgie's after.'

'You'll give me a ring at the gallery to let me know?'

'Yes, I'll give you a ring.'

'Take care then.'

'Look, Mum, I'm just going to school for Chr . . . Pete's sake. What can happen to me at school?' He hesitated, then kissed her cheek. If he hadn't, she'd have looked unhappy and he'd have felt guilty and, and, and it just wasn't worth it, thought Mike as he trudged out the gate, ducking to avoid the honeysuckle on the trellis above. Mum was too short to get a face full of honeysuckle leaves every time she went out the gate. She didn't seem to notice that Mike had grown taller than her.

Do all mothers stress like that, wondered Mike. Or was it just because his mum only had him to stress about.

Mike hesitated on the footpath. The best way to go to school was to duck behind the house and wander along the creek and through the fields. But he was too late for that today. Or he could duck around the corner and up Wallace Street, but that took longer too.

The quickest way was straight down the street then up the Gunyabah road, past Mum's gallery and the post office and supermarket. But that meant going past Lance the Loser's, which meant walking to school with Lance.

The Loosleys lived next door, in an old wooden house like Mike's, with a long garden rambling back onto the creek reserve and fields. But Mum had had their house done up before they moved in, with a new shiny roof and blue and white paint and a second bathroom, while the Loosley's was still rust and sagging steps and cracked tiles on the veranda. Loser was always saying how his dad was going to build a granny flat for a bed and breakfast, or a spa and swimming pool, but somehow it never happened.

Mike glanced at his watch. With a bit of luck Lance had already left, or gone the other way to school, assumed Mike.

Mike began to walk up the footpath. It was a nice street. There was nothing wrong with the street, he thought gloomily. The wide-branched jacaranda trees were just starting to sprinkle their purple flowers on the ground, and the green gardens had solid fences and well-fed dogs . . .

It was just . . . it was just . . . well, what was the point of it, thought Mike. Day after day, always the same — Mum and her fussing, the walk to school and Lance the Loser assuming they were friends just because they'd walked the same route to school since they were in kindergarten. What was the point of school every day, when there was nothing he really wanted at the end of it?

If only something would happen! In a movie, if a kid was walking along a footpath like this, all peaceful and unsuspecting, you'd be waiting on the edge of your seat. The music would be all quiet and tra la la, then suddenly a car would come screaming round the corner blazing bullets, or someone would burst out of the house opposite, and then . . .

'Hello, Michael!' The voice from the Loosley's gateway was soft and warm. Soft like fresh dog droppings and warm as a garbage bag in the sun, thought Mike, as he turned to face Loser's father.

'You're looking very well, Michael,' said Mr Loosley gently.

'Thank you,' muttered Mike. Loser's father always

complimented you, always in that soft, warm voice. If there was ever anything that needed doing in the community Mr Loosley was there, always smiling, always trying to take charge.

You never saw Mrs Loosley around much. She even seemed to scuttle through the supermarket. She was always smiling, too, but her smiles were a bit more fixed than her husband's, as though nailed onto her face.

'Lance is just coming,' said Mr Loosley.

'Oh, great,' said Mike, trying to sound like he meant it.

'I saw your mother at the post office yesterday,' said Mr Loosley, giving Mike one of his warm, wide smiles. One of his front teeth was hooked over the next one. Mike tried not to stare at it.

'She is looking very well. I suppose the gallery's progressing satisfactorily?' Mr Loosley liked long words, too. Why not just say, Is it going okay?, thought Mike.

'Yeah, it's fine,' he said. Mum never talked about how much her gallery made. But she'd suggested they might go to Vanuatu next holidays, or even to Hawaii, so he supposed things were looking good. Sheesh, he thought, going on holidays with your mum. Didn't she *understand*?

'. . . and I hope you'll tell her if she ever needs assistance, she can always call on me,' Mr Loosley was saying. 'I can depend on you to tell her, can't I Michael?'

'Mmm, what? Oh, yeah, sure,' said Mike, tearing his gaze away from the tooth again. He supposed Mr Loosley was hinting he'd like a job at Mum's gallery.

For some reason, Mr Loosley never held onto any job more than a few months, in spite of the fact that he smiled all the time and was so friendly.

'Here's Lance now,' said Mr Loosley. 'Have a good day you two boys. Study hard, won't you.'

'Yeah,' said Mike, as Loser jogged down the steps. Sheesh, thought Mike, the kid even walks like a loser, bouncing along as if his feet were trampolines, wearing those dumb combat pants Samson's the Drapers had on special, and the shaved head that was supposed to make him look tough but looked more like a bruised egg.

'Dumb old Lance, Wears combat pants,' chanted Mike in his head, as Loser galloped down the path. What else rhymed with pants . . . ants? Dance?

Loser shoved his glasses back up his nose, nodded to his father, gave a small wave to his mother's face peering through the curtains, then began to walk beside Mike. He didn't speak till they were past the house.

'What're you doing this weekend?' he asked Mike.

'Nothing much,' said Mike. 'Might go out to Dad's, help him with the hay carting.'

'Like a hand?' asked Loser eagerly.

'Nah, we'll be right,' said Mike guiltily.

It was a lie anyway. Mum was going to drive him and Budgie over to Gunyabah to see *Thrill Kill* at the movies while she did some shopping, leaving Gail in charge of the gallery. But if he told Lance that, he'd want to come too.

And if he told Loser there was no room in the car, Loser would tell his dad, and his dad would volunteer to drive them all in his old bus, and Mum would probably say, 'How kind of you', because then she could spend the day in the gallery without feeling guilty and then . . .

'. . . anyway, I'm going out to Tenterfield,' said Loser carelessly.

'What, really?' asked Mike, surprised. No one he knew had gone out to the old Tenterfield property since it had been sold.

'Sure,' said Loser airily. 'Dad did some work there last week, and they asked me and Mum to have dinner out there too. I've been there every day after school since.'

'How come you never said before?' asked Mike suspiciously. You never quite knew if half the stuff Loser claimed was true. He was always boasting about something. Like the time he said he and his dad had gone pig hunting, and when Budgie asked, 'What with?', he said, 'With my air rifle', and Budgie had cracked up.

'I haven't seen you all week,' said Loser, accusingly.

Mike shrugged. He'd walked the long way all this week, and then there'd been Budgie's after school and cricket practice . . . Loser was too clumsy to be on the cricket team . . .

'What's it like out there now?' he asked.

Some overseas people had bought the Tenterfield property the year before. No one knew exactly who they were. There'd been a lot of rumours in the town when the O'Connell's had sold it, like how it was going to be a religious commune and stuff like that. But no one had turned up there for months, and when someone did it was just a few blokes in suits who'd arrived in a light aircraft.

'Mum said some foreign company bought it as an investment,' said Mike.

Loser shook his head importantly. 'They're doing experiments there,' he said.

'Experiments? No way. Who'd want to do experiments way out there? What sort of experiments, anyway?'

'Just stuff. You know. Test tubes and everything.' Loser kicked at a thistle on the footpath.

Mike snorted. 'I don't believe you.'

'It's true. Look.' Loser knelt on the neat, green grass (old Mr Halliwell mowed his lawn once a week, even the nature strip, and watered it every afternoon) and unzipped his school bag. 'Look.' He handed a test tube up to Mike.

Mike took it warily. It was just like the ones in the science lab at school. But this one was filled with a dark brown powder, with a glass stopper at the end, well taped on as though for extra security. 'What is it?'

Loser hesitated. 'It's a new explosive,' he said at last. 'One drop of that would blow up the entire school.'

Mike snorted. 'You're joking. You wouldn't be carrying it round in your school bag if it could blow up the school. What if you bumped it or something?'

'It needs a detonator,' said Loser quickly. 'There's this other powder that they're working on, except that one's white, and you have to mix them together before they're dangerous.'

'Yeah, sure.' Mike handed it back to him. 'What sort of work did your dad do out there, anyway?'

Loser bit his lip. Mike waited for him to say research chemist or something else impossible, but then he said, 'They wanted him to fix the gutters and do some other stuff.'

'Oh.' It sounded vaguely possible, thought Mike. Even if Mr Loosley never did much work round his own place, Mike supposed he could fix gutters and do other handyman repairs. 'Do they speak English, or what?'

'Japanese,' said Loser.

'How do you know? You can't speak Japanese.'

'Well, it sounded like Japanese,' said Loser defensively.

'They could be Korean or Vietnamese. How did they tell you what they were working on anyway, if they spoke Japanese?'

'A couple of them spoke English.'

'So what are they? A religious group or something?'

Loser hesitated again. 'Yeah, sure,' he said. 'They've got this leader, but he's in prison in Japan . . .'

'You mean like that Japanese group that put poisonous gas in the Tokyo subway?'

Loser nodded. 'Like them.'

'Yeah, sure,' said Mike. 'So they're brewing up poisonous gas outside town, they employ your father and then they ask you and your mum out to dinner there.'

'They did! They did ask me and Mum out to dinner!'

'And they're making poisonous gas?'

'Yes!'

'I thought you said it was explosives.'

'They're doing that too,' said Loser after a moment's pause.

Mike handed the test tube back. 'Well, you'd better look after it.' They were almost at the school now. Groups of young kids bounced through the gates to the primary school playground, pigeons pecked hopefully round the rubbish bins. Mike and Loser headed over the crumbling old bitumen towards the lockers.

'Anyway,' said Loser. 'My dad says . . .'

'Hey, Mike!'

Mike turned and saw Budgie galloping across the road. 'Hey, Mike, guess what's on tomorrow? *Thrill Kill* is on a double bill with . . .'

'I thought you were going out to your dad's tomorrow,' said Lance.

'Yeah, well,' said Mike.

Budgie gave Loser a concentrated look of contempt then walked away. 'Did you get your invitation to Jazz's party?' he asked Mike.

'Sure,' said Mike.

'What party?' asked Loser.

Budgie ignored him. Mike hesitated and said, 'Jasmine's birthday party. It's on Sunday, out on the river.'

'No one told me,' said Loser, then stopped. His face grew red. He pushed his glasses up his nose angrily.

Budgie smiled at him. It wasn't a nice smile. 'Jazz probably made you a special invitation, Loser,' he said. 'I bet it's pasted on your locker now.'

'Was that where your invitation was?' asked Loser.

'Sure,' said Budgie.

'No it wa—' began Mike, then stopped.

'You'd better go and look in case it falls off,' suggested Budgie. 'Jazz would really hate it if you missed her party.'

'I . . .' began Loser. He nodded suddenly and ran off towards the lockers, his long legs flickering like spider's legs in his camouflage trousers.

'There won't be an invitation there,' said Mike. 'Jazz gave them all out yesterday. I thought she was inviting the whole class.'

'Not him,' said Budgie with satisfaction. 'Caitlin told Jazz she'd give Loser his invitation after school, so Jazz gave it to her and Caitlin tore it up.'

Mike stared. 'Why?'

'Because Jazz's new here. She doesn't understand about Loser. Anyway, he's got a crush on her.'

'What's wrong with that?' asked Mike.

'Loser and Jazz? Yuk,' said Budgie.

'You told Caitlin to do it, didn't you?'

Budgie shrugged. 'Sure. But get this — guess what Loser's going to find taped on his locker?'

'His invitation?'

'Nah. A letter from Jazz saying he's the coolest spunk she's ever met and asking him to meet her round the back of the gym before school starts.'

'Did Jazz really write it?'

'Nah, of course not. I wrote it,' said Budgie proudly. 'Come on, we'd better get round to the gym or he'll be there first. Jordie and the rest are probably already there.'

'I . . .' Mike paused. It wasn't that he liked Loser. He didn't. He disliked him and felt sorry for him and feeling sorry for him only made him dislike him more. Loser had no right to make people feel sorry for him.

But all the same . . .

'I've got to take some books back to the library,' he said lamely. 'I forgot to do it yesterday.'

'But . . .' Budgie shrugged. 'Sure, suit yourself,' he said, and ran off.

CHAPTER 2

FRIDAY, 8.35 A.M.

Mike trudged across the tatty tarmac. Already the air was rising in small liquid shimmers above it, thick with the peculiarly school-like smell of old wood, kids and concrete.

School smells hot, of books and rot, said Mike's feet, as they tramped across the tarmac.

It was cooler on the veranda. The thick brick walls were gloomy in winter — all cold-damp and streaked with pigeon droppings where the birds perched and waited for the bell, knowing that it meant a fresh lot of scraps were about to be delivered to the schoolyard — but you were glad of the shade in summer.

It was an okay school, Mike supposed. At least there was plenty of space. The school had been getting steadily smaller for the past twenty years, as the shirt factory on the outskirts of town closed down and then the train line, and lots of families had moved away. There was even talk of closing the high school altogether, which would mean he'd have to bus it an hour each way to Gunyabah every day, or else go and board in Sydney, away from everyone he'd ever known.

What was the point of high school anyway, thought Mike, as his footsteps clattered on the splintery wood. It wasn't like there was anything he really wanted to do after he left school, not that doctor-lawyer-engineer-type stuff Mum was always on about, anyway. Sheesh, imagine being shut up in an office all day without even any school holidays . . .

He turned the corner to the lockers and looked around cautiously. But there was no sign of Loser. He must have grabbed the note and read it, then run straight to the back of the gym.

Mike could just imagine Loser's face when he read it, his silly grin below the owl-like glasses and the shaved head that made him look more like a bald peanut than a tough-guy. No, he wasn't going to feel sorry for Loser. He wasn't.

'Hi, Mike.'

'What? Oh, hi Jazz.' Mike turned and watched as Jasmine's long brown hands shoved her bag into her locker. Jasmine was new in school that term. Her dad was an exchange teacher from England, and her mum had come too, taking a year off so the family could wander round the country in the school holidays. Which meant that Jazz was hardly round at all, thought Mike regretfully. They even seemed to be out at weekends.

Jazz smiled at him, and shoved her hair behind her ears. It was long and black. Like silk, Mike supposed, though he couldn't remember if he'd ever seen anything made out of silk. He tried to think of something to say to her, but his mind seemed to have turned into dog food. Jazz's skin was sort of silky too, he thought, and pale brown like milky coffee. Someone had said that her mum was Jamaican, but Mike's mum didn't think so . . .

'See you,' said Jazz, in her high-pitched English accent. Mike watched her hair sway as she walked down the veranda.

No wonder poor old Loser has a crush on her, Mike thought. He was probably still down behind the gym, waiting for her. When she wasn't there he'd probably . . . he'd probably . . .

Mike's legs seemed to move before he knew what he'd decided. Along the corridor, down the steps, past the tuck shop and round the hall to the small garden behind the gym.

He stopped.

It was like a scene in a video, when you've pressed the 'Pause' switch so you can go and grab a drink. There were the sunflowers, limp and dusty in the hot morning air. There was Loser, his feet in shabby joggers frozen in the dirt, his fists clenched, his face red, his eyes behind his glasses even redder, as though he was going to cry. No, please, please, thought Mike, don't let him cry.

Budgie and Jordie and Fizzer Lucas were there, but they were moving, even though everything else was still. They were laughing — Budgie almost bent over with the giggles, Jordie slapping his back, Fizzer gasping for air he'd laughed so much.

Suddenly Loser moved. His head twisted to look at Mike, then at the other three, and Mike realised he wasn't about to cry at all. His face was red with rage.

'It isn't funny,' he said. His voice squeaked with intensity, which made Jordie laugh even more.

'It isn't funny,' Loser repeated. His voice was louder now.

'Your face!' choked Budgie. 'Mike, you should've seen his face.'

Mike said nothing.

Loser reached into the pocket of his combat trousers. He held up the test tube with the dark brown dust inside. 'You see this?' he demanded. His voice still shook with rage. Or was it pain as well, wondered Mike.

'You got some doggy doo for lunch?' choked Budgie.

'No,' said Loser. His voice was flat now, as though all emotion had drained away. Or maybe there was so much, thought Mike, that he had to push it all away to be able to speak at all. 'It's a . . . a . . . biological weapon.'

'A what?' Budgie's grin grew even wider.

'A biological weapon! Like on TV last week! All that brown stuff is millions of viruses. All I have to do is drop this test tube and you'll all be dead! All of you!'

'Oh, yeah?' Budgie was still gasping for breath. 'I suppose you ordered it on the Internet?'

'No,' said Loser.

'Well where did you get it then?'

'Tenterfield,' declared Loser. 'They've got a lab out there. I went out there for dinner with my parents. I said I was going to the toilet and sneaked into the lab and stole it.'

'Oh, you did, did you?' Budgie made a lunge for it. 'Let's see it then.'

Loser backed away, the test tube clutched to his chest.

'Hey, that's enough,' said Mike. 'Break it up. You've had your joke.'

Loser shot him a glance. Mike had thought he would be grateful, but it was a look of the most concentrated hatred he'd ever seen. He doesn't want to be grateful, thought Mike suddenly. It's easier to hate me too. Just like I don't want to feel sorry for him.

Loser's back was against the gym wall now, with Mike between him and the others. Loser pushed him away. His hands were shaking too much for it to be a hard push, but Mike moved anyway.

Loser blinked furiously at each of them from behind his glasses. 'I'll give you all till break,' he choked. 'You've got to apologise by then. If you don't apologise you're all dead. Dead!' his voice shattered on the final word. He bit his lip, then ran.

Budgie was still giggling. 'Oh, man, you should have seen him,' he said.

'I did,' said Mike. He tried to work out what he was feeling. Anger, he decided. It was Loser's fault, not Budgie's. If Loser wasn't such a try-hard, no one would pick on him. He brought it on himself.

'He was standing there with this goofy look on his face,' hooted Jordie. 'And then Budgie said . . .'

The bell rang, drowning him out.

'Come on,' said Mike, as the echoes died away. 'We'd better run.'

CHAPTER 3

FRIDAY, 9.20 A.M.

There was no sign of Loser at assembly. No sign of him in class either.

Mike tried to switch his mind onto *Henry V*. It was a dumb story, this stupid king pretending he was doing the right thing invading someone else's country and Shakespeare sucking up to royalty and making it seem like he was okay . . .

Loser had probably run off home, he decided. He'd be telling his dad about how they'd persecuted him at school and Mr Loosley would march up to talk to Mr Andrews this afternoon, and in his soft, too reasonable voice demand something be done about the discipline in the school, gangs of bullies out of control and all that stuff, just like he'd done last year, when Loser had been given a detention for hiding under the cypress trees out front and throwing stones at Budgie and Jordie.

Mr Loosley had threatened to write to the newspaper and all sorts of stuff so old Andrews had given in and let Loser off, just like he'd given in when Mr Loosley refused to let Loser stay down a year, because of his 'social immaturity' old Andrews had said.

Mike wondered if Loser might have been happier staying down a grade. Maybe Mr Andrews had been right.

'Michael, if you'd care to join us, the rest of the class is examining page forty-three . . .'

Mike looked up. 'Sorry, Miss Jinsky,' he muttered.

'Now what do you think Shakespeare meant when he said . . .'

All that stuff about the test tube, thought Mike. As though there could really be anything dangerous in the stupid thing — viruses or explosives. It was just a load of bullfrog.

Mike wondered what Loser would do when no one apologised. Because they wouldn't, of course, and Loser would look even dumber than before.

'But what's the *significance* of the tennis balls?' demanded Miss Jinsky.

Jazz's hand went up. 'They meant King Henry was just playing, like a kid. But Miss Jinsky, King Henry *was* just like a little kid! He didn't care how many people were killed as long as he got what he wanted!'

Trust Jazz, thought Mike. He settled back to enjoy the argument.

CHAPTER 4

FRIDAY, 11.00 A.M.

Mum had packed him leftover pizza for morning tea. Mike chomped it wearily.

It wasn't that he didn't like pizza, especially the ones mum made with extra olives and chunks of meatball among the tomato. But sometimes, just sometimes, it would have been good to buy a donut at the tuck shop or something. It was as though Mum didn't even trust him to feed himself without her there.

'Hi,' said Jazz, sitting down beside him and stretching out her long brown legs. 'You coming on Sunday?'

Mike swallowed a bit of pizza the wrong way.

'Glup . . . yeah, sure,' he said.

'Dad's hired this great big marquee in case it rains,' said Jazz. 'He won't be back from the Sydney excursion with Year Five till tomorrow, but Mr Pattinson said he and the boys will put it up for us down by the river. Dad's even borrowed a generator so we can have some music. He wants it to be a sort of "thank you" party, because everyone's been so welcoming.'

'Yeah,' said Mike. He wanted to say, 'Of course everyone has welcomed you. You're that sort of person.' But his tongue wouldn't fit round the words.

'Mum's going to . . .' began Jazz. 'Hey, there's Lance. What's he doing coming out of the classroom? He wasn't in class this morning, was he?'

'What? No. No, he wasn't,' said Mike. He wondered if he should tell Jazz about the incident behind the gym, then decided it was just too difficult.

'He looks sort of strange,' said Jazz, her voice full of concern. 'Like something's wrong.'

'Yeah,' said Mike absently, his eyes on Loser.

He did look different, thought Mike, as he watched Loser trot along the veranda and down the steps, though it was hard to say what the difference was. His face was sort of blank but his back was really straight, like he thought he was acting in a movie or something.

Loser took three steps away from the stairs, and gazed around the school yard, his jaw high as if he was Arnold Schwarzenegger about to take on an entire army, then marched across the tarmac towards the line at the tuck shop.

'What's he . . .' began Jazz.

'Shh,' said Mike. Then he added, 'I'm sorry. It's just that Loser was, was sort of upset this morning. I want to see what he's going to do.'

Budgie turned round just as Loser approached. He nudged Jordie, who was in the line ahead of him. Loser said something, but they were too far away to hear.

But I don't need to hear, thought Mike dismally as Budgie began laughing. I can guess what they're saying.

For a moment, Mike thought that Loser was going to strike Budgie, despite the fact that Budgie was bigger and had his mates around. But he just nodded, his fists clenched, then looked around again.

'He's coming over here,' whispered Jazz. 'What's going on?'

'I'll tell you later,' said Mike.

Loser stomped over to them, then stopped. He glanced at Jazz. His face went red, then white again. He stared at Mike instead. 'Well?' he demanded.

'Well, what?' asked Mike.

'Are you going to apologise?'

'Look,' said Mike, annoyed. 'It wasn't me. I had nothing to do with it! I stopped them grabbing you, remember?'

It was as though Loser could no longer hear anything but the words he wanted.

'You're not going to apologise then?'

'No,' said Mike, still annoyed.

Loser's hot gaze turned to Jazz. 'How about you?' he demanded.

'Me? What about?' asked Jazz, puzzled.

'You know,' said Loser.

'No, I don't.' Jazz looked genuinely confused.

'So neither of you are going to apologise?'

'No,' said Mike.

Jazz shook her head, bewildered.

'All right then,' said Loser. His voice sounded odd, as if it was trapped in an empty tin can. 'You asked for it.

Just you remember! You asked for it!' He marched away, strangely clumsy in his too-wide trousers.

'He's off the planet!' exclaimed Jazz, in her just-like-that-show-on-TV accent.

'Well, sort of,' said Mike. He wondered how much to tell her.

'Why should he go off at me? I haven't done anything to him at all!' demanded Jazz.

'Well,' Mike hesitated. It was a bit like telling tales, but Jazz had a right to know. 'He's going crook because he didn't get an invitation to your party.'

'But I gave his invitation to Caitlin! She said she was seeing him after school. Didn't she give it to him?'

'No,' said Mike.

'Why not?' demanded Jazz heatedly.

'Well . . .' Mike searched for words to explain. 'She doesn't like him . . . no one really likes him much and she's best friends with Budgie's sister and Budgie asked her . . . well, anyway, she didn't give it to him.'

'Blast her,' said Jazz. She bit her lip in annoyance. 'I didn't want to leave anybody out. She had no right . . .'

'Well, anyway, that's mostly what he was upset at you about,' said Mike. 'And Budgie and the others pulled a . . . a joke on him this morning. He's pee-ed off at that too.'

'He looked more than that,' said Jazz, still watching the distant figure of Loser as he disappeared up the stairs. 'He looked . . . I don't know . . . desperate or something. Why don't people like him?'

'Because he's such a loser,' said Mike. 'No, that's not it,' he corrected himself. 'I mean, if he just did dumb things people might laugh at him, but we'd still be friends. It's because he won't accept that he's a loser.'

Jazz blinked. 'I don't understand,' she said.

'He's a try-hard. He's always making himself out to be this great hero, saying things like he's gone hunting wild pigs with his dad over the weekend when everyone knows his dad spent the weekend being a nuisance at the Lions Club barbecue. I mean, his whole family are losers too.'

'Poor kid,' said Jazz.

'It's his fault,' said Mike. 'He does it to himself.'

'Poor kid just the same,' said Jazz.

'Hey,' said Mike, seizing his chance. 'Mum's driving Budgie and me over to Gunyabah tomorrow to the movies. They've got *Thrill Kill* showing . . .'

Jazz wrinkled her nose. '*Thrill Kill*?'

'Yeah, it's got whatshisname in it . . .'

'It sounds like it's all blood and car chases and stuff,' said Jazz.

'No, really, it's supposed to be awesome. I don't suppose you'd like to come too?' Mike tried to calculate. If three of them sat in the back seat and one in the front there'd be enough room . . . 'With a friend or something? Caitlin, maybe?'

'I'm not going to be speaking to Caitlin,' said Jazz grimly. 'How dare she . . . Sarah might like to go. I'll ask her and Mum and tell you after school.'

'Great,' said Mike. He tried to stop the grin spreading over his face. His mouth probably looked like a slice of watermelon, he thought.

Then Jazz grinned back and it didn't matter.

CHAPTER 5

FRIDAY, 11.40 A.M.

It was History after break. Jazz was in the History class, as well as Mike, and Loser and Jordie and Budgie, even though Budgie hated History. There hadn't been any other subject he could take that fitted into his timetable.

That was the trouble with a small school, Mike supposed, as they filed in. You only got a few choices of subjects, not even a language, not that he wanted to learn a language. What was the point? And if there was a choice between History and Food Tech, yuk, well, it wasn't really a choice at all.

He glanced round to see if Loser had come in. But there was no sign of him.

Jazz leant over the aisle towards him. 'Where do you think he's got to?' she whispered.

Mike shook his head. 'He was heading this way. I suppose he's marched off again.'

'What did he mean by . . .' began Jazz, then stopped when Mr Simpson stared at them pointedly.

Mr Simpson was really into history. He was even doing some kind of postgraduate degree on it, and had written about Aboriginal trading links in the Elbow Creek area before white settlement. Mr Simpson wasn't a bad teacher, thought Mike. He supposed even boring stuff was sort of interesting when the person who was teaching you was actually interested too.

Suddenly the door opened. Loser stood there, blinking behind his glasses, as though he'd forgotten how to come inside.

Mr Simpson glanced at his watch. 'You're ten minutes late,' he said, and paused.

He's waiting for Loser to apologise, thought Mike. That's what's supposed to happen. The teacher says, 'You're late', and the kid says, 'Sorry, sir, I was down at the oval and didn't hear the bell', or something like that, and then the teacher says, 'Well, don't let it happen again', and the kid sits down. But it's not going to happen like that. Loser doesn't know how to get it right.

Loser looked up at Mr Simpson, then he looked at the class. He didn't say anything. He didn't move.

'Well, come on in, boy!' said Mr Simpson. 'Haven't you got anything to say for yourself?'

Loser took a step forward and then another one. 'You shouldn't speak to me like that, Mr Simpson,' he said flatly. He blinked, as though trying to remember something, then added, 'My dad says that you should make people show you respect. He says if they don't you should make them. Make them,' he repeated. His voice was firmer now.

'Lance,' said Mr Simpson uncertainly. 'Are you feeling . . .?'

'You're not going to apologise either?'

'Apologise!' Mr Simpson seemed to realise something was wrong. 'Lance, why don't you just sit down and we'll discuss this later . . .'

'No one's going to apologise, are they?' Loser's voice had a hint of desperation now. 'So I've got to make them. That's right, isn't it?' he asked no one in particular. 'You've got to make people respect you!'

He reached into his pocket.

'Lance . . .' began Mr Simpson again.

Loser held up the test tube. It looked just the same as it had earlier, thought Mike, the dark brown powder, sealed against the air.

'Do you know what will happen if I break this glass?' asked Loser.

'No,' said Mr Simpson bewildered. 'Lance, why don't you . . .?'

'You're all going to die,' said Loser with the same blank expression. As if he was trying to recite a movie script or something, thought Mike, but didn't quite know how.

'That's what's going to happen,' continued Loser. 'Everyone in this room is going to die, and then it's going to spread right through the town and everywhere. That's what happens when you let a virus out,' he added, his voice almost like a little kid's telling a fairy story. 'The virus spreads and spreads and you can't stop it. There're lots of viruses in here.' He held the test tube higher.

Mr Simpson moved towards him and stretched out his hand. 'Lance, I think you'd better give that to me . . .'

Lance moved. One step across the room, his arm raised, then PING, the test tube shattered against the table.

The room was still. Loser gazed at their faces. 'Now you'll see,' he whispered. Then he was gone.

The room was silent. Someone giggled at the back. Caitlin, thought Mike. She was the sort who'd giggle at a time like this.

Mr Simpson looked at the mess of glass and brown powder on the floor and table. 'Can anyone tell me what that was all about?' he asked plaintively.

No one spoke. Mike swallowed. 'Loser . . . I mean Lance . . . said he got that stuff out at the old Tenterfield property. He said they're doing experiments out there and he got a test tube of this stuff.'

'Viruses?' asked Mr Simpson disbelievingly.

'Well, that's what he told Budgie and Jordie. But he told me when we were walking to school that it was a test tube of explosives, except you needed white powder to detonate it.'

Mr Simpson's lips twitched. 'Explosives? Biological warfare?' He bent down and rubbed a little of the powder between his fingers. It left a reddish stain, like dried blood.

'I think I know what this is,' said Mr Simpson. 'It's ochre. You can buy it at the hardware store. You add it to concrete when you're mixing it, to change the colour.'

'Loser . . . I mean Lance's dad's been doing some

handyman stuff out at Tenterfield. At least, that's what Lance said.'

'Which is where I suppose he got this from,' said Mr Simpson, 'even if it's not an agent of biological warfare.'

He grinned. 'I think we can assume it's safe to get back to the history of the gold rushes. Someone . . . Caitlin . . . could you run and get a dustpan and brush from the tuck shop? Thank you. Right, where were we?'

CHAPTER 6

FRIDAY, 12.14 P.M.

Mike bit his lip. He hated Friday tests. You thought all the information was in your brain, but as soon as you had to write it down it evaporated.

He glanced across the aisle. Jazz was frowning over her paper too. In front of them Mr Simpson chewed his pen thoughtfully as he bent down to read what Budgie was writing. 'Try to write a bit more legibly, boy,' he muttered, blinking irritably.

Suddenly, he straightened stiffly, as though his back and knees ached. 'Does anyone else find it hot in here?' he demanded breathlessly.

Mike blinked. It *was* hot, but not that hot. No warmer than it had been yesterday, or the day before.

Mr Simpson rubbed his fingers over his forehead, then spread them out and stared at them. His fingers twitched, then twitched again. 'I think . . .' said Mr Simpson slowly. 'I think I had better sit . . .' His voice stopped, but his mouth stayed open. Suddenly he screamed, arching backwards. He screamed again. This time he fell, landing awkwardly on the edge of Budgie's desk. He tried to grasp it, but another spasm struck. He fell to the floor, still screaming.

Someone else was screaming, Mike realised. Caitlin, and a couple of the other girls too. No one moved, but someone had to. Someone had to do something.

Jazz scrambled to her feet. Mike clenched his fists to wake himself up and followed her. They bent over Mr Simpson.

'No,' gasped Mr Simpson, 'no.' He arched and screamed again, his arms and legs flailing against the floor.

'I'll get Mrs Trang,' said Jazz hurriedly. 'I'll tell her to call an ambulance. You'll stay with him?'

Mike nodded. He wondered if he should get Mr Simpson a glass of water. That was the sort of thing they did in movies. But what use could a glass of water be? Maybe he should hold his legs down. Or . . .

The others were crowding around. Mike found his voice again. 'Stand back,' he said. 'Everyone back to their seats . . . no, I mean everyone go to the back of the room. Stand well back. Budgie, you and Jordie move your desk back. Better move the others too.' The ambulance men would need room to put a stretcher down, he thought.

Caitlin said shakily from the back of the room. 'It's the powder, isn't it?'

'What powder?' began Mike, then realised what she meant. 'No, of course it isn't. The stuff in the test tube couldn't have done this. It's impossible. It's just a coincidence.'

Mr Simpson screamed again. His back arched, and his feet and hands drummed strange patterns on the floor. Then as suddenly as it began he was quiet again.

'Mr Simpson?' whispered Mike.

Mr Simpson's eyes opened. 'Can't breathe,' he muttered. 'Can't breathe . . .' His body spasmed again.

Mike sat there helplessly. There must be something he could do. Something! He could hear someone's laughter from another class; far off in the distance, the sound of magpies sleepy with the heat. Normal sounds above the painful breathing of the man on the floor.

'Maybe we should, like, go outside,' said Caitlin nervously.

Mike stared at her. 'Why?'

'Because . . . because if he's caught a virus from that test tube we might catch it too. He might be infectious.'

'There was nothing in the test tube!' said Mike angrily. 'Nothing dangerous anyway. Where would Loser get something dangerous from?'

'He said from Tenterfield,' pointed out Budgie. 'Maybe they're from that sect in Japan.'

'Yeek, I saw a programme about them on TV,' said someone else.

'They made that poisonous gas stuff and killed all those people.'

'I saw it too! The show said the people are still at it,' said Emma Donaldson.

'No, it didn't, it said they might be,' said someone else.

'They had a place in Australia. That's where they made it . . .'

'My dad says a teaspoon of that biological warfare stuff could wipe out the world.'

Suddenly everyone was speaking at once. 'Quiet!' yelled Mike, then bent to Mr Simpson as he began to scream again. 'Can't you be quiet?' What was taking Jazz so long, he wondered. Surely she should be back now!

Someone pounded down the veranda. Jazz burst through the door, then leant against the wall, puffing. 'The ambulance is on its way,' she gasped. 'I explained to Mrs Trang. How is he, Mike?'

'Bad,' said Mike. He glanced down at Mr Simpson. At least he was lying quietly now, though his breath still came in painful gulps.

'Did you tell her about the virus stuff?' demanded Caitlin.

Jazz nodded. 'She said it was probably just Lance showing off. But she said just to be sure we're to cover the rubbish bin with this.' She held up a plastic bag. 'Just so if there is something dangerous in there, no more of it will get out. Then she wants us to go down to the hall and wait there.'

'Is she coming here?' demanded Mike.

Jazz shook her head. 'She's waiting for the ambulance, to show them where to go. She says in case we're infectious we're not to speak to anyone, or go near anyone. Just go straight to the hall and wait there.'

Caitlin began to cry noisily at the back of the room.

'Shut up,' said Mike absently. He looked up at Jazz. 'We can't just leave Mr Simpson here by himself,' he objected.

'Mrs Trang said we have to, just in case. The ambulance will be here soon anyway.'

Mike hesitated. It seemed wrong to leave Mr Simpson all alone.

'Come on!' insisted Jazz.

Mike looked round at the crowded faces. They were waiting for him to say something, he realised. They wanted someone to tell them what to do.

'We'd better take our bags and stuff,' he said finally. 'In case we need anything in them. We've got to go past the lockers in any case. Okay, everyone, gather up your stuff. You go first,' he directed Jazz. 'I'll bring up the rear.'

Jazz nodded. She stepped over to her desk and grabbed her bag and the pen and books off her desk, then headed out of the room. The others followed her.

Mr Simpson jerked again. The seizures were getting stronger now, Mike realised. He tried to think of anything that would cause fits like this, but there was nothing. Nothing. Epilepsy wasn't like this. When that kid in Year Three had had a seizure, it hadn't been like this at all.

'Help me,' muttered Mr Simpson. 'Help me.'

'Help's coming,' whispered Mike. 'The ambulance is coming.' Mr Simpson jerked again. Mike didn't know if he had heard him or not.

The last of the class filed out the door. Mike placed his hand gently on Mr Simpson's shoulder. 'I have to go. They won't be long, sir. I promise.'

Mr Simpson didn't answer.

CHAPTER 7

Mike walked quickly out of the room. Down the corridor, past the lockers . . . he pulled his locker door open, grabbed his bag and the jumper he kept there in case he needed it and headed after the others. The hills shimmered in the distance, framed at the end of the corridor by the blue shadows hovering above the hot brown fields.

Past the Year Nine Maths class, the faces peering at him curiously, down the stairs, over the hot tarmac to the hall . . .

The door was open. Mike went inside.

It was a large hall, built when the school had had twice the number of students it had now. There was a stage at one end, with long black curtains pulled aside, and a piano just below it. On either side of the stage were toilets, male and female, then a long expanse of scratched brown floor till the stacked chairs at the end. Under the high windows the walls were pockmarked with years of posters and art competitions, each leaving a Blu-Tac stain or bit of yellowed tape to show where they'd been.

The class had spread around the hall. People were standing in twos or threes, or even alone. Mike wondered how many of them had realised that the person standing next to them might be infected, that if they stood too close, their best friend might infect them, too.

Jazz had dumped her bag on the stage. She came up to Mike. 'I'm going to ring Mum,' she said.

'But won't that just worry her? I mean, Mr Simpson might be sick with something else.' He tried to think how his mother would react if she thought he might have been exposed to some virus, and shuddered. She'd insist on coming down and taking his temperature or something embarrassing . . . 'How can you ring her, anyway?'

Jazz held up a mobile phone. 'Mum's a doctor,' she said briefly.

'I didn't know,' said Mike.

Jazz shook her head. 'Mum said not to tell anyone. She wanted to take a year off. She's not registered to practice in Australia, but she thought, since there's no doctor in town, people might expect her to anyway. It just seemed simpler not to say anything.'

Mike nodded slowly. The regional Health Service had been advertising for a doctor for more than a year, and the Council was trying too. But no one seemed interested in coming way out to Elbow Creek. The nearest doctor was at the hospital at Gunyabah, and when he went on holiday or got sick there was no one at all.

'Your mum's Jamaican, isn't she?' he asked hesitantly.

'Ugandan,' said Jazz, swinging her dark hair behind her. 'Mum and her family escaped from Idi Amin.'

Who was Idi Amin? wondered Mike. The name was sort of familiar. He wanted to ask what it was like in England if you had brown skin, but he couldn't think of a way to do it.

'Better duck into the girls toilets to make the call,' he suggested instead. 'Then they won't all be listening or want to use the phone too.'

'They can borrow it if they like,' said Jazz. 'I don't mind.' Then she shook her head. 'Actually, I'd better save the batteries. We might need it later.' She slipped the phone back into her pocket and headed towards the toilets.

Mike wandered over to the chairs. His feet echoed in the empty hall, clung, clung, clung. He grabbed a chair and set it upright, then dumped his bag on it as Budgie walked over to him.

'Did the ambulance come?' he asked.

'I don't know,' said Mike. 'It hadn't when I left.'

'Loser couldn't have done that to Mr Simpson, could he? Not really.'

'I don't know,' said Mike slowly.

'Nah. It's impossible,' said Budgie, a bit too firmly. 'Guess what?'

'What?'

'Caitlin's writing her will.'

'Her will? What's she got to leave in a will?'

Budgie snorted. 'Her Barbie doll collection maybe. I dunno. It could just be a goodbye letter or something.'

Mike glanced over at Caitlin. She was sitting hunched on the floor, her back to the wall, with what looked like her English notebook on her knee. She wrote furiously for a moment, paused, frowned, chewed her pen, then made a face and went back to her writing.

'There's probably nothing at all to worry about,' said Mike uncertainly. 'He just got sick with something else . . .'

'Sure,' agreed Budgie. 'I wonder how long they'll keep us here for?'

Mike tried to think. 'Well, if it was the stuff in the test tube that affected Mr Simpson, it worked pretty fast. So if any of us are going to get sick it probably won't take long. But it's all impossible!'

It had to be impossible, he thought. Death didn't just seize you from an empty sky. Biological warfare and mass murder had no place in real life. It was just pretend. There was no way it could be real.

Budgie let out a long breath. He looked at his watch. 'It'll be lunchtime soon,' he said. 'I hope they remember to get us something to eat.'

'I've got sandwiches and stuff in my bag,' offered Mike. 'You can share if you like.'

Budgie shook his head. 'I want a hot dog and a packet of crisps,' he said. 'But thanks anyway.'

'That's okay. Come on, let's grab some chairs. We may as well try to get comfy.'

CHAPTER 8

FRIDAY, 12.50 P.M.

Jazz came out of the toilet. Her face looked damp, as though it had just been washed. Mike wondered if she had been crying, but she tried to smile as she came over to them. 'Mum said not to worry, just to sit tight,' she said.

'Jazz's mum's a doctor,' Mike told Budgie.

Budgie looked affronted. 'I didn't know that.'

'She's not supposed to practice here. We didn't tell anyone.' Jazz hesitated. 'She said that it's really hard to make proper biological warfare stuff, much harder than people think. Either the virus dies before it goes very far or it kills the person carrying it. She says Mr Simpson probably has food poisoning or something. There's nothing really to worry about.'

Mike shook his head. 'It didn't look like food poisoning.'

'You're not a doctor,' said Budgie.

'Yeah. But it still didn't look like food poisoning.'

'There's different types of food poisoning,' said Jazz.

'See?' said Budgie.

'Sure, but . . .' Mike shut up. It wasn't worth it.

'Hey, what's that noise?' Budgie crossed the room and peered around the door. The others followed him.

'We're not supposed to go outside,' Jazz warned him.

'I'm not. I'm just looking. Hey, everyone's getting out of class.'

Caitlin shoved her way to the front of the group. 'But the bell for lunch hasn't gone,' she objected. 'They're all going out the front, like you know, a fire drill or something.'

'Evacuating,' said Mike. How come they're all evacuating if there's nothing to worry about, he thought. But he didn't say it. 'Come on,' he said to Caitlin 'We'd better get inside.'

'Oh, go jump,' said Caitlin crankily. 'Like, who made you boss, anyway?'

'No one,' said Mike. 'I just think . . .'

'I'll do what I want to!' Caitlin's voice was high and tight. Mike had never heard her speak like that before. It must all be really getting to her.

'If I want to stay here I will. I can . . .' Caitlin's voice trailed away. 'It's hot,' she said more quietly. 'I think I will come inside. Not because you told me to.' Her voice grew sharp again. 'Just because I want to . . . I want to lie down.'

Jazz took her arm. 'Caitlin, are you okay?'

'I don't know. I feel . . . funny. Everything looks sort of greenish. Like shadows . . . My knees, my knees won't work.'

'Yes, they will,' said Jazz soothingly. 'Come on, come inside and lie down. Mike, have you got a jumper or something she can use as a pillow?'

'Sure,' said Mike. He grabbed his jumper and brought it over to them.

'I don't want your jumper. I just want . . .' Caitlin shuddered and she began to pant. 'My hands,' she gasped. 'My hands feel . . . feel like . . .'

'Come on, just lie down for a bit,' said Jazz comfortingly, but her eyes met Mike's anxiously.

'I . . . I . . .' began Caitlin. Suddenly her body arched. She fell. Her mouth grinned in a long and terrifying scream, over and over and over . . .

No one moved. It was impossible to move, thought Mike. It was impossible that any of this could be happening.

Suddenly Jazz stumbled forward. She reached a hand out. The movement brought Mike out of his daze.

'Don't touch her,' said Mike sharply.

'But . . .'

'Don't you understand?' cried Mike. 'We have to keep away!'

Jazz looked at him strangely. 'You mean if I touch her, I might die too? But we've probably already been infected. We're already going to . . .' Her voice broke.

We're going to die, thought Mike. It's true, it's really true. We're going to die. The thought pounded through his head, yelling at him, screaming at him.

How could it have come to this, he thought desperately. It shouldn't be like this! It shouldn't be like this at all . . .

'Get back,' he choked out to the others. 'Everyone get back.'

'I'm going to ring the front office,' said Jazz. 'Maybe the ambulance is still here.' She fumbled for her phone and began to dial. 'Could you connect me to Elbow Creek Central School front office please? Yes, it's in Elbow Creek. What? No, it's near Gunyabah. Look, it's really urgent . . .' Then, 'Miss Clancy? It's Jasmine Fallerton in the hall. Caitlin's . . . Caitlin's sick. It's like Mr Simpson. Yes. Yes. Please hurry. Oh, please hurry . . .'

Caitlin began to scream again.

CHAPTER 9

FRIDAY 1.10 P.M.

'I'll kill him,' said Budgie. 'I'll really kill him. You just watch me.'

'Yeah,' said Jordie. 'But not straight away. We'll . . .' he hesitated as he tried to think of something suitably horrible to do to Loser, then caught Jazz's eye. His voice trailed off.

'Lance was holding the test tube when it broke,' said Jazz quietly. 'He was right next to it, even closer than Mr Simpson. He must have breathed some of it in. Maybe no one will have to kill him at all . . .'

No one said anything. Suddenly Emma gave a high shrill hiccup and buried her head in her hands. 'We're going to die,' she whispered. 'We're all going to die!'

'Shut up!' said Mike fiercely. 'No one's going to die! They've taken Caitlin and Mr Simpson to hospital haven't they? And they're not dead yet!'

'But they might die!'

'They're not going to!' repeated Mike. Sarah put her arms round Emma. Emma gave a small choked sob and shuddered against her shoulder.

They had all crowded at the other end of the hall as the ambulance men in masks and white boiler suits slid Caitlin onto a stretcher, and carried her out.

'You'll be all right, kids,' one of the men had said reassuringly. But his eyes above his mask were worried.

Jazz's phone rang. She pulled it out and pressed the button. 'Hello? It's Mum,' she whispered, then held it close to her ear again. 'Yes, we're okay. No, no one's hysterical.' She put her hand over the mouthpiece again. 'Mum thinks we're all really brave,' she reported. Mike grimaced. None of them were really brave, he thought. But they were all friends. Even those who didn't really like each other were friends, in a way. You had to be in a small town, or else you became an outcast, like Loser . . . Mike thrust the thought away.

People in the city could wait for other people to help them. But in the country you need your friends. If there was a fire or a storm or a flood you all pitched in. He wondered how a group of strangers would have coped, all cooped up together in a situation like this.

Mike bit his lip. Had any other group of kids anywhere in the world ever been in a situation like this?

'Did you get hold of Dad?' asked Jazz into her mobile. 'Yeah, I know it takes ages to get back here, I just wondered . . . no. Yes.' She held the mobile away from her ear again: 'Hey, has anyone got a pen and paper? I need to write this down.'

Mike rummaged in his bag and handed her his history notebook and a biro.

'Thanks,' said Jazz. She balanced the notebook on

her knee and began to write. 'Okay, Mum, go on. Right. Right. Yeah, I've got that too. Yes. Love you too, Mum. Bye.'

Jazz put the phone back in her pocket. 'Mum says she's organised fresh clothes for us. That's in case any of the powder got on our clothes. She's got surgical masks for us too. Someone is going to push them through the door on a trolley in a few minutes.'

She consulted the notebook, and looked up at the group again. 'Mum said we're to go into the toilets, one by one, and take off all our clothes and put them in the plastic bags they're sending too,' she reported. 'Then we're to wash all our exposed skin with soap and wash our hair as well. We're not to take the new clothes out of the bags until we've dried ourselves and we have to seal the bag of old clothes up before the next person comes in. Is everybody clear?'

There were nods around the room. 'Mum said . . .' Jazz drew a deep breath. 'Mum said we're not to share any food or drink either. Just in case. Any questions?'

'Are they sending shampoo too?' asked Sarah.

Jazz shrugged. 'Don't know,' she said.

'I hate him.' Emma's voice was low and hard. 'I hate him, I hate him, I hate him. How could he do this to us!'

The words echoed around the half-empty hall. No one answered.

'Hey, how about we all just get undressed here?' said Budgie helpfully. 'It'd save time.' He leered half-heartedly at Emma.

Mike tried to grin. Budgie was just trying to lighten things up.

'In your dreams, Budgie Williams,' said Emma, wiping her eyes with a soggy tissue. 'Who goes first?'

Mike swallowed. 'Those who were closest to Caitlin,' he suggested. 'Sarah, you'd better go first.'

'So had you,' said Jazz quietly. 'You were holding Mr Simpson's hand.'

'Okay,' said Mike.

'Coming through now, kids!' yelled a voice outside. The doors opened as the trolley slowly rumbled through.

CHAPTER 10

FRIDAY 1.25 P.M.

It wasn't easy washing in a handbasin, but at least Jazz's mother had remembered to put in towels. Mike pulled on the clean shirt, then tried to work out how to tie the mask. It felt ridiculous, he thought, glancing in the mirror. Yep, it looked ridiculous too.

He waited for someone to laugh as he came out of the toilet, but no one did.

'Your turn,' he said to Budgie.

Budgie was only gone five minutes. Mike wondered how thorough he'd been. But at least he wore his mask. Then Jordie, Darryn, Sam. On their side of the hall the girls were coming out one by one, clean and masked too, their wet hair straggling around their necks or tied up in dark, damp ponytails.

The phone rang again, diddly diddly ding ding ding. Mike watched Jazz answer it. He wondered if she could change the ring. The tone was beginning to get on his nerves.

She'd changed into jeans and a T-shirt in the toilet, and her long black hair was pulled back with some pink fluffy thing. The mask looked very white against her skin.

Budgie plonked himself down next to Mike. 'You know, it's funny,' he said. His voice was slightly muffled through the mask.

'What?'

'All this. I mean, if you saw it all in a movie or something it'd be exciting. But it's not. It's boring. I mean, we're all scared but it's boring, too.'

Jazz pushed the button to end the phone call and sat down beside them. 'You mean killing's a thrill on TV but not in real life?' she said with a touch of savagery. 'Boys! All you ever like is shoot 'em ups and car chases. You never give a thought to the poor old spear carriers.'

'The what?' asked Mike

'Spear carriers. You know, those people in the movies who just hold a spear as the emperor walks past, then get stabbed when the hero escapes.' She snorted. 'Boys only seem to like the sort of movies where half the onlookers get killed. You know, by the time the hero finally catches the bad guy fifty people who just happen to be passing by have been shot or squashed in the car chase or . . . or you know what I mean.'

'Hey, we're not all like that,' protested Mike.

'Oh yeah? What was the movie you planned on seeing tomorrow?'

Mike was silent.

'Well, now we're in the movie, and it isn't exciting at all,' said Jazz.

Mike wondered if other girls thought like that, but

didn't have the guts to ask. That was one of the things he liked about Jazz. She was interesting. 'What did your mum say?' he asked, to change the subject.

'Not much. Dad's on his way back here with Year Five, and she can't reach him. Caitlin's still . . . still alive, and so's Mr Simpson. They gave them oxygen in the ambulances. Mum asked . . .' Jazz took a deep breath. 'Mum asked if I'd like her to be with us in here, or do what she can to help outside.'

'What did you tell her?' asked Mike.

'I said help organise outside.'

'I thought she wasn't allowed to do anything?'

'I don't suppose it matters at a time like this,' said Jazz.

'Hey, look at this!' Mike looked up. Jordie was standing on a chair, peering out one of the high windows. Budgie leapt up to join him.

'Look!' said Jordie. 'There's all these SES people in orange uniforms down the road. There's a barricade too.'

'I suppose that's to stop anyone coming near us,' said Mike. He supposed Mum knew all about it by now. She must have if she'd sent his clothes. She'd be frantic . . .

'Do you want to ring your mum?' asked Jazz, as though she'd read his mind.

Mike shook his head. 'Maybe later. Like you said, we need to save the batteries.' He leant back against the wall. 'I wonder what Loser's doing. If he's okay? He must have breathed in that stuff too. Do you think they're looking for him?'

'Yes,' said Jazz. 'If . . . if it is infectious, he could be spreading it all over the place. I'll ask mum next time she calls. I suppose the police have sent someone out to that place too. What's its name?'

'Tenterfield. There's only Constable Fielder and Senior Constable Svenic, and Constable Fielder's on leave. He's taken his family up to Surfer's for a fortnight.'

'How do you know?'

'His wife works for mum on the weekends. But I'd probably know anyway. Most people know most things about everyone in a town like this. You'll find out.'

'I suppose.' Jazz leant back next to him. 'You know, I didn't think I'd like it here. But I do. It's funny though. Back home I was a black kid, but here I'm lighter than most of you. I mean, Fizzer and Jordie are Kooris and they treat me like I'm white. It feels sort of odd.'

'Where do you come from in England?'

'Manchester.'

'What's it like?'

'Dirty. Noisy. Lots more happening there than here, but mum and dad mostly won't let me do it if it means being out by myself at night. I don't know . . . you can stretch out here. Breathe. I know it sounds silly.'

'No, it doesn't,' said Mike.

'What do your parents do?'

'Dad's got a farm out of town. I don't see him much. They split up when I was just a kid. Mum's got the gallery in town.'

'I know it. Dad said he wondered how a gallery makes a living in a town this small.'

Mike shook his head. 'The gallery's just a sideline. Mum mostly works on the Internet. She imports stuff and sells it to other galleries around Australia and sometimes she acts as an agent for artists and craftspeople and sells their stuff for them too. She does okay.'

'You the only child?'

'Yeah.'

'Me too. It makes you want to scream sometimes, doesn't it? All that attention focused just on you.'

'I suppose,' said Mike slowly. He'd never thought of it that way.

'Sometimes I wish my mum and dad had had ten kids. But other times . . .' she shrugged. 'It's not bad being spoilt.'

Budgie plonked down next to them again. 'What the hell are the police doing?' he complained. 'They must've caught Loser by now.'

'Even if they have that won't help us,' Mike pointed out.

'Yeah, but it'd make me feel better if I thought he was getting what's coming to him.' Budgie stood up again and kicked the chair. 'It's all this waiting! If only they gave us something to do!' He mooched off again.

Mike and Jazz watched him go. 'Do you want me to ring mum again and see if there's any news?' asked Jazz.

'You said we had to save the batteries,' said Mike.

'They can give us a charger. Or another phone,' said Jazz. She began to press the buttons. 'Mum? It's me. No, I'm fine. Really and truly. No, I promise, I'll call you at once if . . . Really, we're fine at the moment . . . Look, I just wanted to know if they'd found Lance yet?'

She paused as she listened. Mike looked round the

room. A bunch of girls were whispering in the corner; most of them had been crying, their faces still held the traces of tears.

The boys were scattered around the hall in twos and threes, some in masks, some still waiting their turn. None of them seemed to be saying much.

'But that's crazy . . .' said Jazz into the mobile. 'Can't they . . . yeah, I suppose. No, I told you, everyone's okay for now. Just bored. There's nothing to do here. Yes, all right, we're scared but we're handling it. Yes, I love you too. Mum, don't go on like that, it's embarrassing. Yes. Yes. Talk to you later.' She pushed a button to end the phone call.

'Well?' demanded Mike.

'They can't find Lance.'

'He didn't go home?'

'No. And Mr Loosley's furious. He says it's impossible that Lance ever took a test tube. He says someone must have planted it on him to make him look guilty. He says . . .'

'But that's crazy,' interrupted Mike.

'I know. He says Lance was never out of his sight at Tenterfield and that they didn't go anywhere in the house except into the kitchen.'

'I bet,' muttered Mike.

'And he's threatening to sue the police and the school and everyone for defamation and child abuse and wants every other kid in the class arrested for hassling his son and . . . and I don't know what else.'

'Crazy,' said Mike again.

'But he doesn't know where Lance is. No one does. He just seems to have disappeared.'

Mike tried to think where Loser might have gone. Down the creek behind the house? But they'd have looked there for certain. The park? The milkbar?

Surely they'd have searched all those places. What if he'd collapsed somewhere and . . . Mike tried to push the thought away. 'Did anyone go out to Tenterfield?' he asked.

'They haven't had time yet. Mum said that Constable Svenic thinks he ought to stay here, so he rang Gunyabah and they're sending someone out.'

'But that'll take ages!' Mike protested.

'Mum said they'll radio in as soon as they get there.'

'Yeah, great. Meanwhile we're stuck here waiting for . . .'

Suddenly the hall doors were flung open. Another trolley slowly emerged through them, followed by the dumpy figure of Mrs Trang in the blue dress with red piping that she wore every Friday in summer, and probably had for the last hundred years, thought Mike. But this time she wore a white mask over the lower part of her face as well. 'Would one of you boys please give me a hand!' she called in her quiet, precise accent.

Mike scrambled to his feet. 'Mrs Trang, won't you be infected if you come in here?'

'No, I am sure I won't,' said Mrs Trang, just a bit too reassuringly. 'I am sure there's no danger at all. It is probably just a form of food poisoning.'

Then why are you wearing a mask, thought Mike. But he didn't say anything.

'Has someone else in town fallen sick then?' demanded Jazz.

'No. No, they haven't.' Mrs Trang brushed her grey hair back nervously. 'But I am sure . . .' Her voice trailed off behind the mask. 'I would like some help, please,' she said more briskly. 'We need to unload this.'

Mike pulled off the cover.

'A TV!' exclaimed Budgie.

'It's a video,' corrected Mrs Trang.

'Cool. Hey, what movies did you bring?' Budgie demanded suspiciously. 'Not Walt Disney stuff or anything?'

Mrs Trang smiled. You couldn't see her mouth but you knew it was a smile, thought Mike, because of the way her eyes wrinkled up. 'No,' she said. 'One of the Year twelve boys picked the videos for me.'

'Great,' muttered Jazz in Mike's ear. 'It'll be all . . .'

'Yeah, I know,' whispered Mike. 'Car chases and shoot 'em ups.'

'Mrs Trang?' said one of the girls.

'Yes?' said Mrs Trang.

'Are they going to send some doctors or something for us? So we won't get sick?'

Mrs Trang hesitated. 'Well, it's all taking longer than we thought,' she admitted. 'Constable Svenic was called out to a property outside the town early this morning. It took a good deal of time for the emergency people to contact him. Then he had to contact the Council, and the Council had to contact the State Emergency Service, though Mrs Allen tells me that half of them were here already, as they had already heard about it from someone else.'

Mrs Trang sighed. 'It all took a great deal of time,' she said. 'Constable Svenic finally contacted the HAZMAT unit at Warilla in Wollongong about an hour ago, that's the hazardous materials unit . . .'

'Wollongong!' exclaimed Mike. 'But that's thousands of kilometres away!'

'They should have sent out a unit from the nearest regional centre to us,' continued Mrs Trang, 'but they thought Constable Svenic said Gunnedah not Gunyabah . . . and, well, no one is here yet.'

'So they haven't even tested the stuff in the test tube yet?' said Jazz slowly.

'No. Constable Svenic is trying to arrange a flight to get it to the Analytic Laboratory at Epping in Sydney. But even when it gets there it will take them at least twenty-four hours to give us a result,' said Mrs Trang shortly.

'But that's crazy!' began Jazz

'I know,' said Mrs Trang. 'But there is nothing any of us can do except wait and hope the authorities manage to get organised before . . .' Her lips closed with an almost audible snap. 'Now can one of you please set up the video? There are some drinks and sandwiches here as well, and some fruitcake and, well, many other things, I think, in those containers. The CWA has set up an emergency canteen just past the barricades.'

'At least *they've* got their act together,' muttered Mike.

'Are you staying with us?' asked a girl at the back of the group.

'Yes,' said Mrs Trang gently. 'I will be staying with you.'

CHAPTER 11

FRIDAY, 1.55 P.M.

The sandwiches turned out to be corned beef and tomato, egg and lettuce, and ham and yellow mustard. The fruit cake was packaged stuff from the supermarket, dry and uninteresting, but there were home-made chocolate chip and peanut biscuits, too, the ones that Mrs Halloran contributed every time the CWA had a stall outside the newsagents on Saturday morning, and chocolate slice with coconut on top that looked home-made too.

Mike wondered if the chocolate slice had been made specially for them, if someone had heard there'd been a disaster at the school and immediately run in to the kitchen to start cooking, cooking, cooking, the only thing they knew to do to help.

There were fruit boxes, too, and cans of soft drink and bottles of spring water and someone had thought to add a box of tissues, which Mike reckoned would be useful if some of the girls started crying again.

He wished he could cry. He would, he thought, if he

were by himself. But not with Budgie and Jordie and the others watching. Mike swallowed the lump in his throat. Yes, it would have been good to be able to cry.

It was impossible to eat with masks on. So everyone found a place where they wouldn't breathe on someone else, and tried to force food down.

Mike sat where he could see a slice of daylight and concrete through the door. The world was normal out the door. Somewhere, cattle were sleeping in the thin shade of gum trees; somewhere even further off kids were doing schoolwork or gazing out the window, never dreaming of what was happening so far away in a school like this.

How long would it take for their worlds to go back to normal, Mike wondered suddenly. If Loser really had released some kind of biological warfare thing, what was to stop it from spreading all over town, and then to the next town, then to Sydney maybe, and then across the world?

Maybe the virus, or whatever Loser had in the test tube, was already blowing in the breeze outside. They were all crammed in here for nothing, and people outside would start getting sick . . .

Mike glanced at his sandwich and forced himself to take a bite. It was important to eat, Mrs Trang had said, though she didn't say why. Mike supposed it was just one of the things adults said. Or perhaps when you were hungry you got light-headed, and when you got light-headed it was easy to get hysterical and that was the last thing they needed now.

'It's hard to eat, isn't it?' asked Jazz.

Mike started. He hadn't noticed her walk over to him. He nodded, and wrapped the sandwich back in its plastic.

'I'll finish it later,' he said.

'It all seems crazy, doesn't it,' said Jazz, leaning back in her chair.

Mike nodded. 'I keep thinking, out there everything is going on like it always does. Then I wonder, for how long . . . it just doesn't seem right that things can be sort of normal, then bang, you're in the middle of something like this.'

'That's what Mum said about Uganda,' said Jazz slowly. 'She was at school and everything was fine — well, as far as she knew anyway, she was just a little kid. Then suddenly people wanted to kill her because she was from the wrong tribe, her parents were from the wrong tribe. The knives came out all over the city,' she said. 'I never asked mum what she meant by that. I've never felt I could.' She hesitated. 'I've never told anyone else about mum saying that that,' she admitted. 'I used to have nightmares about it when I was small. All the knives and the darkness, and this little kid watching . . .'

Mike felt a warmth seep through him. He wanted to say something, something that would show he understood, that would show he wanted to know all the other things that had marked her life, had made her the Jazz that sat beside him. But all he could think to say was, 'Yeah.'

'Why do people kill each other!' cried Jazz softly. 'I just don't understand! Don't they realise that life is precious! People even watch other people being killed and they enjoy it!'

'What . . .' began Mike, visions of really weird behaviour in Manchester before him.

'On TV!' elaborated Jazz fiercely. 'People watch people being shot and stuff on TV and they think it's fun!'

'But . . .' began Mike. He wanted to say, 'Only because it's not real. It wouldn't be fun if it was real.' No one ever killed anyone for fun . . .

Or did they? Were there places in the world where people really did enjoy killing? Did Loser . . .

No, thought Mike vehemently. No! Whatever Loser had felt when he smashed the test tube, it hadn't been pleasure. There'd been pain on his face, not enjoyment. Pain so great that all he could do was lash out because he couldn't bear it any longer . . .

'You know what I think?' asked Jazz softly.

'What?'

'I think some people are makers and some people are destroyers. Some people create things or help other people, and others just take what they can. I think we have to choose which one we'll be.'

'What about my mum,' said Mike, confused. 'She doesn't make things. She just sells stuff that other people make.'

'But she helps them to do it when she sells it,' said Jazz. 'Your dad's a farmer, isn't he? He creates things.'

Mike was silent. Suddenly the thought of the corn slowly growing in the soil out at the farm seemed the most peaceful thing in the world. And the bright yellow of the oil-seed rape, sort of shouting its colour to the sky.

Mike wondered suddenly if Jazz had ever seen a field of corn in flower. When he was small, he'd always thought he would be a farmer, too. But now . . . well, sometimes it seemed like dad didn't think he was his son any more since he'd moved into town with mum. You had to have a farm to be a farmer . . .

'Okay!' called Mrs Trang. 'Which video do you want to watch first?' She began to read out the titles.

'*Persuasion*!' yelled Sarah.

'Nah, chick's movie,' objected Budgie.

'It is not!'

'Yes, it is. All they do is talk all the time.'

'*Titanic, The Phantom Menace* . . .'

'Seen it,' called someone else.

'We could see it again . . .'

Mike took no part in the discussion. He didn't really care what movie they chose, as long as it kept them all absorbed, took their minds off reality just a little bit. He just wanted to be far away, somewhere he didn't have to feel or think about this situation any more . . .

Jazz's mobile rang. 'For heaven's sake, can't you make it sing another tune?' snapped Mike, before he thought about what he was saying.

Jazz looked at him in surprise as she pressed the button to answer it. 'Sure,' she said. 'I'll change it to "Happy Birthday", if you like. I think it does the "William Tell Overture" too . . . Yes, Mum?'

The hall grew silent as she listened. 'Sure, Mum. Yes, I'll tell them. What! What do you mean they can't . . . but that's impossible! I mean, it's really lunatic. Yes, I know. Yes, I know it's not your fault. Yes. Love you. Bye.'

'What is it?' asked Mike urgently.

'There isn't anyone out at Tenterfield.'

'They must have gone back to Japan or Korea or whatever,' said Mike. 'Did they find any lab stuff when they searched the place?'

'They didn't search the place,' said Jazz grimly.

'But . . . but why not?'

'Because they didn't have a search warrant.'

'But this is an emergency . . .'

'But it's not officially an emergency yet. It won't officially be an emergency till the State people declare it one. The local people here can't seem to do that.'

'But that could take hours!' protested Budgie.

Jazz shrugged. 'Don't blame me. I'm just the messenger. That's what mum told me, too. Not to blame her . . .'

'Did she say anything else?' demanded Mike.

'What? Oh, yes. The SES have rounded up some mobile phones for us. They asked everyone they knew who wasn't part of the operation or . . . or related to us if we could borrow their phones. Mr Morelli at the newsagents lent them his and the people at the cafe too and they made an announcement to the Senior Citizens. Some of the old people have mobile phones in case they fall down or something. They all agreed to lend them — there's one for each of us. The SES have asked our parents to stay at home, so we can call them.'

'That's kind,' said Mrs Trang softly. 'People in this town can be so kind.'

'She says we can talk as long as we like, and they'll reimburse people, somehow, for the bill. They're sending the battery chargers in too, but we'll have to take turns at the power points. She suggested we all ring our parents first, just so they know we're okay. Then if we want to ring friends or anyone we can.'

'Who will you ring first, Mrs Trang?' asked Mike, without thinking.

'No one, I think,' said Mrs Trang in her quiet voice. 'My husband and my daughters died on the trip out here. I have no one I . . .' She shook her head. 'It is best I think perhaps if I keep my phone free, in case the other phones are tied up, in case someone needs to contact us urgently.'

Mike stared at her. He'd known in the back of his mind that Mrs Trang had come from Victnam. That was why she still had an accent. But it had never occurred to him that she'd been a refugee, that perhaps she'd known horror before this.

Surely she's had her share of terror already, he thought. But she still volunteered to stay with us.

'Perhaps I will ring some friends tonight,' added Mrs Trang, smiling at him earnestly behind her mask.

'Do you think we'll still be here tonight?' he asked.

'Perhaps,' said Mrs Trang honestly. 'Yes, Michael. I think perhaps we will be.'

CHAPTER 12

FRIDAY 2.10 P.M.

'Oh, Mike, do take care.'

Mike sighed. It was the tenth time at least that his mum had said that. 'Mum, I'm taking as much care as I can. It's not like I'm swimming with crocodiles or something. I'm just sitting here.'

'What else are you doing?'

'Watching a video. Sort of, anyway.'

'Which one?'

'*Titanic*. Does it matter?'

'No. I . . . I'm just talking for the sake of talking, I suppose. You'll call me at once if . . . if anything happens?'

'Yes, Mum,' said Mike. 'I promise I'll call you.'

He mentally crossed his fingers as he said it. If anything did happen, if another one of them got sick, he didn't think the first thing he'd be doing was ringing his mum.

'I love you, Michael.'

Michael glanced around, but everyone was speaking into his or her phones too. No one seemed to be listening to him. 'I love you too, Mum,' he said quietly. 'See you soon. Don't stress. There's nothing to stress about. Really.'

'Nothing to stress about!' his mum's voice choked with what was almost laughter. 'Oh, Mike . . .'

'Love you, Mum,' said Mike again, and pressed the 'Off' button.

He leant against the wall and shut his eyes.

CHAPTER 13

'Jazz?'

'Mmmmm?' Jazz turned away from the window she'd been peering out of and looked down at him.

He was getting used to her wearing a mask, Mike realised. It was funny how fast you got used to the unthinkable. 'I just wanted to say I'm sorry,' he said. 'For snapping about the phone like that.'

'What? Oh, that's okay. No worries,' Jazz added in what Mike supposed she thought was an Australian accent. She stepped off the chair and sat down on it instead. Mike sat down next to her.

'I keep thinking about Loser,' he admitted. 'It's funny that in spite of everything I still hope he's all right. I couldn't say that to Budgie and the others though. They'd think I was crazy.'

'I don't think it's crazy,' said Jazz slowly. 'Lance has to be sick, that's all. There's no other reason for him to have done this.'

'You mean mentally sick? Insane?'

'Not insane. But mentally sick, yeah.'

Mike shook his head. 'That doesn't make sense. Loser knew what he was doing. Do you think everyone who does bad things just does it because they're sick in the head?'

'Yes. No. I don't know,' admitted Jazz. 'Something as bad as this though . . . being sick's the only answer that makes sense.'

'I think some people are just born bad,' said Mike.

'You mean Lance has been bad all his life?'

Mike thought about it. Loser was just . . . well, a loser. He'd never really done anything evil before. Even when they were just little kids, playing in the creek behind their houses, Loser had been okay.

'You know something,' said Jazz softly. 'I don't think Lance even knew what he was doing was real. I think he was all caught up in a movie in his head. None of us were real to him, just like the spear carriers in a movie aren't real. Okay, so they fall down dead. But we all know they're actors, and when the movie's over they get up again. You don't cry for spear carriers.'

'So we're the spear carriers now?' asked Mike.

'I suppose.' Jazz blew out her breath in a long sigh, sending her mask billowing outwards. 'I just wish something would happen, even though I'm scared of what it might be. I hate waiting,' she admitted. 'I even hate waiting at the dentist. I want to get it over with.'

'Me too,' said Mike.

'I was trying to imagine myself somewhere far away from here. It didn't work though.'

'Back in England?'

Jazz looked surprised. 'No. Down by the river actually. You know, I'd never seen a river like that before I came here.'

'It's pretty small,' said Mike.

'But it goes such a long way. Right down to the Murray eventually, then down past Adelaide and out to sea. It looks like it knows it's on a long journey, you know what I mean?'

'Sort of,' said Mike.

'It's really cool,' said Jazz dreamily. 'Sort of slow, with all those deep pools and the sand just lying there in great big waves, and you don't have to worry about pollution or anything.'

'Dad's property's on the river,' said Mike. 'There's a spot where we go fishing sometimes.'

'What's it like?'

'It's this great bend. There's a big rocky cliff on the other side, and sandy banks where we fish. The river's really deep there.'

'Do you catch anything?'

'Sure. Yellow belly and Murray cod if you're really lucky. I caught one at nearly four kilos last year.'

'Did you eat it?'

'Sure. Well, most of it. I brought it home for mum, and she gave some of it to the Kennedy's next door. It was too much for the two of us.'

'I've never tasted Murray cod,' said Jazz. 'Have you rung your dad yet?

Mike blinked. 'Dad? I didn't think . . . I mean, no, I

haven't. He wouldn't be near a phone till knock-off time anyway. He probably hasn't even heard of any of all this yet.'

'He will soon though,' said Jazz. 'I bet it'll be on the news and everything.'

'Yeah, I suppose,' said Mike slowly. 'I didn't think of that.'

'You don't see him much?'

'Not much. I don't think . . . I mean, he never seems all that eager to see me.'

Jazz made a face. 'Men!' she said.

'What do you mean?"

'I bet you don't seem very keen to see him either, so he thinks you're not keen and you think he's not keen.'

'It's not like that . . . well, maybe. Women act like that, too.'

'No, we don't,' said Jazz. 'We scream at each other. We don't hide away.'

'I'm not hiding . . . look, I'll ring him later, all right? I bet Mum's already tried to get through to him.'

Jazz grinned. She looked strange behind the mask, thought Mike, but it was definitely a grin.

'Boy, you're bossy,' he said.

Jazz grinned even wider. 'So are you,' she pointed out.

'Yeah, I suppose so.' Mike felt a grin tugging at his lips too.

'Mike?'

'Yeah?'

'If . . . if all this ends well, what do you think you'll be doing in ten years time?'

'In ten years? I don't know,' said Mike slowly. The image of fields of ripening corn rose in his mind, but he dampened it down.

'Where will you be? Will you still be here?'

'I suppose. To be honest I don't know what I want to do after school. Uni, I suppose. That's what Mum expects me to do anyway. I just don't know. How about you?'

'I want to study medicine,' said Jazz.

'Like your mum?'

'Well, yeah, but not because she's a doctor. I just like the idea of it.'

Of course, thought Mike. Jazz would have to be a giver, not a taker. 'It's hard to get into,' he said.

'I know,' Jazz hesitated. 'I'll make it,' she said. 'Does that sound really full of myself?'

It did, a bit, but Mike said, 'No.'

Jazz grinned again. 'You know . . .' she began.

'Mrs Trang!' cried Sarah. 'Quick! It's Emma! Quick!'

CHAPTER 14

FRIDAY 3.00 P.M.

Someone yelled something outside, one of the SES volunteers perhaps, too far away to make it out. It sounded like an instruction or something, thought Mike, with a small part of his brain. The rest of his mind focused on Emma, lying on the floor of the hall, with Sarah kneeling beside her.

Mrs Trang hurried over. 'Jazz, get on the phone to your mother,' she called over her shoulder. 'Sarah, how is she?'

'She says her tummy hurts,' said Sarah anxiously. 'And she feels hot and she's got a headache.'

Jazz pressed the buttons on her phone and spoke into it briefly while her other hand rummaged for the pen and notebook in her pocket. Mrs Trang knelt beside Emma and took her hand. 'All of you are to move well away, right down the other end of the hall. You too, Sarah.'

Sarah shook her head stubbornly. 'She's my friend. I want to stay,' she said.

Mrs Trang hesitated, then she nodded. 'Yes, then. You can stay,' she said. 'Emma, can you hear me? Can you speak?'

Mike moved slowly down to the end of the hall. His feet felt frozen cold, even in the growing heat of the hall. For a moment he wondered if he too might be sickening with whatever it was, but it was only shock, he realised, shock or terror or pain, because Caitlin and Emma were his friends, and even Mr Simpson was part of his life, too.

There was a commotion at the other end of the hall. Mrs Trang gave what sounded like a giggle, a slightly hysterical giggle, but still a giggle. She got to her feet and helped Emma up and they moved across the hall to the girls toilets.

Sarah stood up too. 'It's all right,' she called. 'It was a false alarm.'

'What's wrong with her?' demanded Budgie.

Sarah hesitated. 'Just her period,' she said shortly. 'She had stomach cramps, that's all.' Suddenly she began to laugh. Her eyes filled up with tears. She laughed as though she didn't know how to stop. 'I'm sorry,' she gasped through her tears. 'I'm sorry. I don't know why I'm laughing. I could strangle her. I mean, she's my friend and all that, but honestly.' The laughter choked her again.

Jazz shoved the phone, pen and notebook into her pocket and moved swiftly over to the drinks trolley. She fished out a can of lemonade, flicked it open and handed it to Sarah. 'It's shock. Relief,' she said. 'Here, drink this. Go on. You'll feel better.'

Sarah nodded. She took a sip and then another. She sniffed and wiped her eyes. 'Thanks,' she said. 'Thanks, Jazz.'

Jazz nodded without speaking. Mike watched as Budgie moved over to Sarah. They sat down together by the stage and began talking in low voices.

Jazz walked back to Mike and sat down on the chair next to his. She seemed to remember something and fished out her phone again. The pen fell to the floor and she picked it up absently. 'Mum, are you still there? No, I know you're not going anywhere. It's all okay. She's got her period, that's all. Is Dad back yet?' She paused and listened. 'Yes, Mum. Yes. Love you too, Mum. Give my love to Dad. Yes, I know I'll be speaking to him soon, but . . . bye, Mum. Bye.'

She leant back against her chair. 'Mum was really stressing,' she said. 'I suppose it's hard on her too.'

Mike looked around the room. Just about everybody was sitting in groups of twos or threes now, as though there was more reassurance in a smaller group. Or maybe, he thought, deep in our hearts we're waiting for the next person to get sick, and don't want to be sitting next to them. At least we're together, he thought. Loser was alone . . .

'What are you thinking?' asked Jazz.

'What? Oh, nothing much. About Loser again. Wondering what's happened to him.'

'Why do you call him Loser?'

Mike shrugged. 'His surname, I suppose. Loosley, Loser. He's always been Loser, as long as I can remember.'

'It's cruel,' said Jazz.

Mike blinked. 'Well, I suppose . . . I mean he is a loser. He just can't do things right, but he's always pretending he's better than everyone else. His dad's like that too. Always saying how brilliant his son is, making him study all the time, but Loser's never been much good at anything, no matter how hard he works. Mr Loosley says it's all the school's fault, and if Loser was at a better school he'd do really well, but it isn't that . . . No one likes any of them much, but his dad is always pretending they're really close friends with everyone. Like he always says, "Say hello to your mother for me", but Mum can't stand him.'

'That's even sadder,' said Jazz.

Mike was silent. He supposed to an outsider it would seem cruel. But Jazz didn't know them like he did.

'Maybe you can feel sorry for Loser,' he said at last, 'but not for Mr Loosley. I was at their place one time. I mean, they live next door so I used to go over sometimes. They've got a big yard, just like we have, but they've got chooks down the back of their yard . . .'

'Chooks?' asked Jazz.

'Hens. You know, chickens. Well, this dog had got into the chook, I mean, the hen yard, and killed a couple of them. Loser and I heard all the noise and raced in and pulled it out. It was a cattle dog, grey and white and sort of stupid. It wagged its tail at us like it had done something really clever.'

'Yes?' said Jazz.

'Well, Mr Loosley came out. He saw what the dog

had done but he didn't say anything. He just went into the shed and brought back this bottle of poison. He called out to Mrs Loosley to bring him a bit of meat, no please or anything. So she brought him out some mince and he poured a bit of this white stuff onto it and called out to the dog, "Here boy", really gently. That's how he always talks, sort of quietly.'

'What happened next?'

'I let the dog go,' said Mike. 'I was only a little kid. I didn't want to. I mean, I sort of knew what was going to happen. But he was a grown-up, so I let the dog go and it bounced up to him and ate the mince from his hand, all sort of happy like it was being given a treat,' Mike stopped.

'Yes?' said Jazz softly.

'It died,' said Mike. 'It didn't take very long. Mr Loosley just stood there watching it, smiling all the time. Then he looked at me and said, "Well that should prevent it killing hens, shouldn't it, Michael?" I didn't ever go there again,' he added.

Jazz chewed the pen thoughtfully. 'Do you think that because Mr Loosley killed a dog, Lance might kill people?'

'I hadn't thought of it like that,' said Mike. 'No . . . no . . . yes, because it wasn't just that he killed the dog. It was because he smiled, because he didn't even feel sorry for the dog, or try to find its owner. It's like nothing else matters to him, like he's pretending so hard to be nice there's no room to feel anything for other people. I don't know,' he added helplessly. 'It's just, you can't trust them. They pretend.'

'Maybe they wouldn't pretend if people really liked them,' said Jazz. She sounded annoyed, thought Mike.

Mike snorted. 'I bet they'd just pretend even more.' He shook his head. 'What really gets me, though — I mean, Mr Loosley's nasty. Really bone-deep nasty. But Loser . . . well, he's just a loser. All that stuff about the test tube . . . first he says it's an explosive and then it's filled with viruses. I mean, whoever those people out at Tenterfield are, they wouldn't leave stuff like that lying around for people to pick up. I wonder if they've managed to get the test tube down to Sydney yet?' he asked Jazz

'I told you, Mum said it's on its way,' said Jazz impatiently.

'No, you didn't,' said Mike.

'Yes, I did. I'm sure I did.'

'You didn't,' said Mike.

'Look!' began Jazz, then she stopped. 'Maybe I didn't. I'm sorry. I've . . . I've got a headache . . .'

'Jazz?' said Michael softly.

'What?' She met his eyes. 'Mike . . . I'm scared,' she whispered. 'I've got a . . . a sort of headache. It's getting worse. And my chest feels funny, like it hurts to breathe.'

'Ring your mum,' said Mike quietly.

'No. Maybe it's just a headache . . .'

'Ring your mum,' ordered Mike. 'Or I will . . .' He took out the mobile phone he'd been given and tried to remember how to work it. 'What's her number?'

Jazz told him. 'It's probably nothing,' she whispered.

'Mrs Fallerton? I mean, Dr Fallerton, it's Mike. I'm in the hall with Jazz. She's not feeling well. No, I haven't told Mrs Trang. Jazz doesn't want to. Yes, I'll put her on.'

He handed the phone to Jazz. She fumbled for a moment, as though her hands were stiff, then held it up to her ear. 'Mum? It can't be the same thing. The others were screaming. They kept jerking around . . . No, it's just a headache. A really bad one. Everything looks sort of green. It's just like I can't be bothered to move or breathe, everything feels so stiff.' She listened for a moment, her eyes wide and frightened in her mask. 'Mum, no,' she whispered. 'All right then. I'll be there . . .'

She handed the phone back to Mike. A tear rolled down her cheek, hit her nose, then dribbled invisibly onto the white mask. 'Mum says to go and sit by the door,' she whispered. 'She says they'll have a stretcher there in a couple of minutes. She says the ambulances aren't back yet, but one of the SES men has offered . . . they've fixed up a station wagon.' She stopped and gasped for air.

'Come on,' said Mike. 'I'll help you over.'

'No! You shouldn't get too close!'

'Shut up,' said Mike, near to tears. He put his arm around her waist and helped her up. It was funny, he thought absently. He had dreamed what it would be like to touch her, but not like this.

He was vaguely aware of Mrs Trang's phone ringing, of her answering it and ordering the others to stand back. She came over to them and put her arm around

Jazz's other side. She only came up to Jazz's shoulder. 'You should have said something,' she said, but her voice sounded pained, not angry.

'I didn't realise . . . I was hoping . . .' whispered Jazz. 'Mike, Mike, my knees won't work . . .'

'It's all right,' said Mike. 'We've got you. It's all right. We're nearly there.'

Together they helped Jazz over to the door, then lowered her to the floor. Mike looked around uncertainly for something to use for a pillow, then sat next to her and put her head on his lap. Her hair was dry now, and tangled, but it still looked like silk.

'I'm scared,' whispered Jazz.

'It'll be all right,' said Mike helplessly. 'You'll be fine.'

'Jasmine!'

Mike looked up. He had only ever seen Jazz's mother in the distance before, but she was unmistakable, even taller than her daughter, with the same dark hair and eyes, but darker skin.

Mike had thought she looked like a model the first time he saw her. Now she wore a too short SES orange boiler suit that she must have borrowed, and her eyes above her mask were scared.

She was accompanied by a man in SES uniform. He, too, was masked, but Mike recognised him. It was Pete the tiler who'd redone their bathroom. He carried a stretcher. He nodded at Mike and Mrs Trang, then put the stretcher down.

Dr Fallerton knelt down beside Jazz. 'Jasmine! Jazz, darling, how are you? No, don't try to talk. It seems to make whatever it is worse if you try to talk. Just lie still. We're going to roll you over . . . as gently as you can, Peter . . . that's right.'

'Please,' said Mike. 'Can I carry the other end?'

Dr Fallerton shook her head. 'No. I can manage.'

'But, please . . . let me come with her.'

Dr Fallerton looked at him properly for the first time. Her tone grew more gentle. 'No, I'm sorry . . . Mike, isn't it? The risk of infection is too great.'

'But I've caught it now if I'm going to!' exclaimed Mike urgently. 'Please! We've been together all day!' He glanced down at Jazz, but her eyes were shut.

Dr Fallerton hesitated, then shook her head.

'But she'll have to go all that way by herself!'

'I'm going with her,' said Dr Fallerton. 'I'm sorry, Mike. I'll ring you if there's any news. I promise.' She and Pete the tiler picked up the stretcher and began to move off.

Mrs Trang touched Mike on the shoulder. He waited for her to say, 'Jazz will be all right. Don't worry.' But she didn't say anything.

Mrs Trang knows things don't always turn out all right, thought Mike vacantly. She knows that even if you love someone, it's not enough to keep them safe.

They watched the stretcher disappear behind the main office, then turned back into the hall. 'You're a good boy, Michael,' said Mrs Trang unexpectedly.

'Thank you, Mrs Trang,' said Mike.

CHAPTER 15

FRIDAY 3.25 P.M.

Mike sat down in the corner furthest from the stage. He didn't want to talk to anyone. He didn't want to see anyone. He wanted to run away, as far as he could, as fast as he could. He wanted to shut his eyes and when he opened them everything would be changed; he'd be back in yesterday . . .

'Mike.'

Mike opened his eyes. Budgie stood in front of him, his mask on crooked, his hands in his tracksuit pockets. 'Mike, she'll be okay,' he said.

Mike shook his head. How could she be okay, how could any of them be okay? He stared at Budgie. Suddenly he was angry. 'It's all your fault!' he shouted. 'If you hadn't played that dumb trick on Loser, none of this would have happened!'

He broke off. Everyone was looking at him. But no one came over. As soon as he stopped talking they huddled back in their own small worlds of fear.

Mike looked up at Budgie, waiting for him to yell back,

to say it wasn't his fault or it was Mike's fault too, or . . .

But Budgie just thrust his hands deeper into his pockets and said, 'I know.'

Mike stared. 'You know?' he repeated dumbly.

'Of course I know. How do you think that makes me feel?' said Budgie flatly. He crossed the hall and stood by the doors, looking out.

Mike sat there. Of course it was Budgie's fault. But . . . but . . . when you really thought about it, it was everybody's fault. His fault, for not stopping them, maybe everyone in the whole class' fault for not being more understanding.

If people treated him like they'd treated Loser, maybe he'd have done the same, thought Mike. Maybe, finally, he'd have been hurt so much that he would have just lashed out and tried to hurt as many people as he could, so they might feel an echo of the pain he felt inside, to hurt his tormentors . . .

No, thought Mike suddenly. No matter how much he was hurt he wouldn't do that. Look at Mrs Trang. She'd been hurt a million times more than Loser had. But she hadn't tried to kill people in return. She'd volunteered to stay with them instead. Kids who weren't even related to her, kids who laughed at her accent sometimes, or the way she got so upset if you weren't super polite.

When you really thought about it, you couldn't blame other people for anything you did at all.

Budgie was still standing by the door. Mike touched his shoulder.

'Yeah?'

'It wasn't your fault, mate,' he said.

Budgie shrugged.

'No, really,' said Mike. 'It . . .' He stopped. It *was* Budgie's fault, but in some way he couldn't explain, it was everyone else's fault too. He'd had it all clear in his mind, but there was no way he could put it into words. He was tired of thinking, tired of feeling. He'd had to think and feel too much . . .

'Come and watch the video,' he said instead. 'Mrs Trang's going to put another one on.'

Budgie nodded. 'Thanks,' he said without turning round. He stood there silently for a moment and then he said, 'I'm still going to hang his guts from a gum tree.'

CHAPTER 16

FRIDAY 3.45 P.M.

It was impossible to watch the TV screen. Mike wasn't even sure what the movie was about. Some chick who liked a guy . . .

At least there were no car chases, thought Mike. At least there were no heroes chasing bad guys through the crowded streets, not caring how many died on either side, as long as they got their villain. 'We're the spear carriers now,' said Jazz's voice in his mind.

Mike shut his eyes. There was no point watching the video. All he could see was Jazz's face as they carried off the stretcher. He hadn't known that brown skin could look so white, that Jazz's bright face could look so blank . . .

Terror gripped him. All at once he was sure that she was dead. She'd died on the ride to the hospital and he would never see her, never. Everything that was once Jazz was gone.

Mike grasped his phone and tiptoed down the hall. He turned his back and dialled.

'Dr Fallerton, it's me. It's Mike.'

'. . . Mike . . .' said the tinny voice from the phone. The sound was broken up. It must be almost out of mobile phone reception range, thought Mike.

'Please . . . how's Jazz?'

'. . . tremors . . . not as bad as the others yet . . .' said the voice. Dr Fallerton was crying, Mike realised. It wasn't just that the line was breaking up.

'She's still alive?' he whispered, then wished he hadn't, because Dr Fallerton began to sob into the phone. He tried not to imagine her, alone except for the driver with her daughter lying in the back of the station wagon, the strange empty fields all around her.

'. . . not even any oxygen, nothing I can do . . . if only . . .' Suddenly the line grew clearer. They must have come up on top of a hill, thought Mike. '. . . if only they knew what it was, we might have some idea how to treat . . .'

'How long till they get the results on the stuff in the wastepaper basket?' he asked.

'. . . don't know . . . all so far away . . .' said the sobbing tinny voice. 'Oh, if only we knew what it . . .' The voice broke off. The line went dead.

Mike dialled again frantically. The phone rang once, twice, and then was answered, 'Hello, I'm sorry I can't come to the phone right now. If you'd like to leave your name and telephone number . . .'

Mike put the phone down. Out of range, he thought. He looked at his watch. It would take them at least half-an-hour to get to Gunyabah. Half-an-hour before he could ring again . . .

He sat with his head in his hands. If only they could get hold of Loser! But maybe Loser had sickened too . . . and even if they did get hold of him, he wouldn't know what was in the test tube. Just that it killed people, and he'd used it.

There had to be some way to find out what it was in the test tube. There had to be!

He had to *think*! If he thought hard enough he'd find the answer; if he thought hard enough he wouldn't think of Jazz lying on the stretcher, her legs twitching just like the dog that Mr Loosley killed . . .

Mike sat very still. Was it . . . could it be . . . he had to think this through . . .

Point number one: Loser had seemed deadly serious this morning. The blank hard look had changed his face, as though he wasn't really seeing any of them any more.

Yes, Loser had looked like he really meant to kill.

Point number two: Loser had said that the test tube held explosives, and then he'd changed his story. Mike had been sure he'd been lying both times. All of them had been sure that he'd been lying.

What if they'd been right?

Point number three: There was something in Mr Loosley's shed that killed . . .

If something could kill a dog, it could poison human beings.

Mike stood up. He walked slowly over to the group watching the video and caught Budgie's eye. He signalled. Budgie nodded, and came across to join him.

'What's up?' he whispered. 'Hey, you're not feeling crook are you?'

Mike shook his head. 'No, nothing like that. Look, I just had an idea.'

'What?'

Mike sat down, Budgie sat next to him. 'Look, suppose there was nothing dangerous in the test tube. What if Loser was just spinning us another of his stories?'

'Yeah?' said Budgie.

'But he really wanted to get at us. And he knew where his dad kept some poison.'

Budgie's forehead wrinkled. 'So he poisoned Mr Simpson and Caitlin ... and Jazz. But how?' he demanded . 'You think he might have put something in their food?'

'I don't know,' said Mike. 'I just don't know. I mean, it'd be different if Loser had passed around a ... a box of chocolates or something. But look, Mr Loosley does have poison in his shed. I saw it.'

'When?'

Mike hesitated. 'Years ago,' he admitted. 'I was just a little kid. But I bet it's still there.'

'Do you want to tell Constable Svenic?'

'I don't know.'

'Why not?' demanded Budgie.

'It's just ... well, you know Mr Loosley. If Constable Svenic turns up at his front door asking if he's got any poison, Mr Loosley's going to say, "No", isn't he? And then if Constable Svenic starts looking, the next thing he'll do is get rid of it, or signal to his wife to get rid of it, and then we'll never know what sort of poison it is. And we have to find out! If we knew what it was then maybe the doctors could do something.'

'Constable Svenic could just sneak in there.'

'He won't,' said Mike decidedly. 'He wouldn't do something like that without a search warrant, just like he wouldn't break into Tenterfield.'

'But what else can we do?' demanded Budgie.

'I'm going to try to find it myself,' said Mike.

CHAPTER 17

FRIDAY, 4.10 P.M.

The window in the boys' toilets was small and high, with narrow glass slats.

'We could break them,' said Budgie helpfully.

'Someone might hear. And if they saw the broken glass they'd know what had happened. No, let's try to get them out. Give me a leg up, would you?'

Mike clambered up onto a basin, then reached across to the window, steadying himself with one leg in Budgie's cupped hands.

'Hold still!' hissed Mike.

'Gawd, you're heavy.' Budgie tried to brace his hands with his knee. 'How's that?'

'Better. I think I can . . . yeah!' he said triumphantly, as the glass slid into his hand. 'Got it . . . here take it, will you?'

'With what? My mouth? You'll have to get down for a sec . . . okay, let's get the next one.'

One slat, two, three, four, five . . .

Budgie looked at the window dubiously. 'D'you think you'll fit through?'

'Yes,' said Mike, more confidently than he felt. 'Come on, hoist me up again.'

'One . . . two . . . three!' said Budgie.

Mike got his head through the hole. 'Damn!'

'What?'

'My shoulders won't fit.'

'Twist them round . . . sort of diagonal,' suggested Budgie.

'I can't. They won't,' grunted Mike, when suddenly they did. Budgie pushed Mike's legs helpfully from below.

'Not so fast. I'll fall!' hissed Mike. 'Sheesh, I don't know how to do this. I'm climbing out head first. Haul me back again.'

'But . . .' began Budgie

'Just do it!' hissed Mike. 'No, wait a sec, I'm going to try to sit up . . . got it . . . now if I stand I can grab the roof . . .'

'But . . .' began Budgie.

'Don't you get it? If I run along the building someone might see me. But if I'm on the roof, the angle will hide me from the road.'

'Just hurry up then!' ordered Budgie. 'Someone might come in . . .'

'Yeah. Sure. I . . .' Mike held on to the top of the window with one hand. The roof was level with his chest now. If only he could haul himself up onto it. He grabbed hold of the guttering and pulled.

The guttering sagged in his grasp.

'Sheesh . . .' Mike grabbed again. This time he felt

the sharp tin edge of the roof properly. He balanced for a moment on the window, then heaved upwards with his hands.

Up . . . up . . . the tin pressed into his stomach, the sagging guttering bulged into his legs. Then suddenly he was there.

'Made it!' called Mike softly. 'Stall them as long as you can, will you?'

'I will,' said Budgie's voice from below. Almost at once Mike heard a low grating noise as Budgie began to replace the glass.

Mike looked around. In the far distance he could see Mount Gunyabah, shimmering purple in the afternoon light. Fields and fences and the stark shadows of thistles and grey clumps of sheep looking like rocks, or rocks looking like sheep, and all around him was grey as well — the concrete of the school, the grey metal roof.

The roof was hot, even now in the late afternoon. It smelt of last year's dust and this year's pigeons. Mike stuffed the mask into his pocket and took a cautious step.

Boom. The iron roofing flexed under his feet, sending not so much a sound as a shudder through the roof.

Sheesh! Double sheesh! Mike froze. It was impossible that someone inside wouldn't hear him, that the sound wouldn't bring someone from the SES as well.

Maybe they'd just think it was the roof contracting now the sun was behind the trees. He took another step, moving as softly as he could. This time the boom was quieter, but still loud in the shimmering air.

It wasn't going to work. Someone would hear him for certain and as soon as they'd got round the corner they'd see him too. It all looked so simple when the hero did it on TV, thought Mike. They ran across a roof as softly as a cat, or else a helicopter conveniently happened to fly by and picked them up, and no one ever looked up and saw them. In real life someone would be sure to see you, unless you slithered on your stomach like a snake . . .

Like a snake . . .

Mike sank to his knees, then lay down flat. The corrugated iron pressed into his knees and stomach. It would be impossible to wriggle on this. Impossible to cross the roof unseen. Every part of him would end up bruised.

It was impossible that Jazz lay in the back of a station wagon speeding to the hospital, impossible that Mr Simpson and Caitlin lay dying too. This was a day for the impossible. He had to try . . . for Jazz's sake. For his own. Mike began to move.

One leg, then the other leg, up like he was swimming, one arm up and then the next. It was slow, incredibly slow . . .

Boom. The roof flexed again.

Then suddenly he heard it. A burst of gunshots, then yelling, then more shots. A car's brakes screamed.

Budgie had turned up the video. Mike grinned, then grimaced as the roof cut into him. He inched around the corner, then on impulse peered over the point of the roof.

He could see the roadblock now and the orange uniforms of the SES. The road was empty. There must be another roadblock even further along, he realised.

Would they be patrolling the rear of the school too? He glanced the other way — no sign of orange uniforms. They wouldn't be worried that someone might approach the school across the fields, only from the road in front.

Would they see him run across the field to where the houses started? If only there were more trees, he might dart from tree to tree. But there were only tussocks of grass. You couldn't hide behind a tussock. There was nothing to hide behind at all.

Except the fence. If he lay flat and inched along the ground he'd be mostly hidden by the bottom rail. Not quite hidden, of course, but if no one was really staring in that direction, he should be safe.

Michael wriggled over to the edge of the roof, grasped the gutter in his fingers and slid over the edge. For a second he dangled there and then the gutter began to bend under his hands. He let go quickly and dropped to the ground.

Pain shot through his ankles at the shock. Just what he needed now — a broken or sprained ankle. But then the pain diminished. Mike peered around the corner again.

No one in sight. They'd all be keeping as far away as possible. Mike darted over to the toilet block, then edged around it. Now for the fence.

The ground was hard as he pounded across it. Every moment he expected to hear someone yell, 'Stop!', but the world was silent except for the magpies, warbling in the trees beyond, and the distant sound of more gunshots from the video . . .

Made it! Mike realised his hands were shaking. He tried to steady his breathing as he slipped over the fence, then lay back down again on his stomach.

Faded crisp packets, grubby lolly sticks, shreds of wild turnip and thistle — the wind seemed to have gathered them all together against the fence. He briefly wondered how many dogs had visited there too. Then he began to slither.

Ten metres, twenty metres . . . he must be in open sight of the front of the school by now, but he didn't dare look up to see. Thirty metres, forty . . . another few metres and he'd be behind the Prothero's tall wooden fence.

Suddenly a dog began to yap.

'Shut up,' muttered Mike. What if someone came out to look and saw him?

The dog kept yapping. Mike kept crawling.

Ten metres now . . . five . . . three . . . Mike reached the cover of the Prothero's backyard fence. It was made of tall wooden palings, bleached grey by years of sun, stained at the bottom by generations of dogs.

Mike stood up carefully. He could no longer see the school or the road. He hoped that meant that no one there could see him either.

The dog kept barking.

He began to jog along the backs of the houses. Paling fences, colourbond fences, there were wire fences too, but no one seemed to be looking out their back windows, or lingering in their gardens. On the other side of him the fields stretched flat and almost lifeless, the long shadows of the scattered gum trees turning black in the afternoon light.

All at once the barking grew frenzied. Mike peered over the fence.

The dog was small and white, with hair that looked like it had been teased out of a ball of wool. It stopped barking as it met Mike's eye and sat on its haunches.

'Woof,' it said hopefully.

'Hello, boy,' said Mike softly. 'Are you bored?'

'Wurruffuf,' said the dog.

'I'd really appreciate it if you'd shut up,' said Mike. ''Cause if you keep making a racket someone's going to come out and investigate.'

'Wrowff?' said the dog.

Mike looked around carefully. The house was one of those old wooden ones, with a bathroom and laundry tacked on the back. The back door was shut, and there was a dog's water bowl in the shade of an old tree by the clothesline. He was pretty sure there was no one about.

'Sorry, boy, but I've got to go,' said Mike.

The dog erupted in a howl of barking. It backed away, still barking, then raced over to the house and disappeared round the side. Suddenly the barking stopped.

Hell, thought Mike, it's gone to tell its owner there's a burglar out the back.

Suddenly the dog reappeared, galloping as fast as its short legs could carry it. It was holding something in its mouth, almost too large for it to carry. It dropped it triumphantly next to the fence and sat on its haunches again.

'Wurrrrurf,' it announced happily.

'You dumb dog,' said Mike staring at the food bowl at his feet. 'I haven't got any dog food! You'll have to wait till your owner comes home.'

'Wurruff? Wuff!' said the dog.

'Great guard dog you are,' muttered Mike, as he started to trot along the fence again. 'Some burglar arrives and you bring him your food bowl. I bet I could break in and steal the whole houseful and you'd be happy as long as I put a few Meaty Bites into your dish.'

'Wurf,' agreed the dog, prancing along the fence next to Mike.

Mike paused at the fence that divided the dog's house from next door. 'Look,' he said to the dog. 'I can't play with you now. But when this is all over, I promise I'll ask your owner if I can take you for a walk. All right?'

'Wuurrruff,' said the dog. It gave a half-hearted spurt of barking as Mike ran on, and then was silent.

CHAPTER 18

FRIDAY, 4.40 P.M.

Things felt better after talking to the dog, thought Mike, as his feet pounded along the rough track behind the houses, worn by generations of bicycles and scooters and gardeners dumping lawn clippings.

Silly little hairy dog, sang his feet against the ground, how he'd like to have a . . . what rhymed with dog, he wondered. Frog? Log?

The dog was such a normal thing, such an everyday thing. Suddenly the world looked like it always did — the dip and slope of tin roofs, the dull-leafed trees and leggy clotheslines and bright plastic little kids' wading pools in the backyards, the mutter and excited music of a game show on someone's TV set behind the curtains.

Right, thought Mike. All he had to do was cut along the backs of the houses till he came to the creek. Then if he snuck along among the willow trees he could come up behind his place and Loser's.

Mike hesitated. If he went in through Loser's back gate Mrs Loosley might be looking out of the kitchen window and see him, or Mr Loosley might be feeding the chooks or something. Of course, they were probably both out looking for Loser, but he still couldn't risk it.

No. What he needed to do was sneak up into his own garden. Then he could climb over the fence right next to the shed and there'd be no chance of the Loosley's seeing him at all.

Mike glanced at his watch: 4.45. On a normal Friday, Mum would still be at the gallery. She usually picked up a couple of pizzas on her way home. Mike always got a couple of videos on the way home, one for him and a not too bad chick-flick that Mum might like as well. He watched the first till she got home, then they watched the next one as they ate . . .

For a moment a longing ran though him — so, so deep it made his bones ache. There'd be no videos tonight and no pizza either.

Suddenly the vision of Jazz lying so still on the stretcher flashed into his mind. Mike ran faster.

Past the rest of the houses, over the sun-hard ground, its gold grass like thin tufts of hair. The creek smelt like it always did; half of sheep and half of too-still water, with the almost-pepper scent of willow trees and rotting wood.

It was harder running here, though he didn't have to worry about anyone seeing him. The creek narrowed then pooled; broken branches lay propped against the trunks, their heads decaying in the water. It was almost like hurdling in athletics, except on the oval there weren't rabbit holes or unexpected puddles. A red-bellied black snake looked up, startled from its perch on a log in the last of the sunlight, then slipped soundlessly down the log and disappeared between the roots.

His footsteps sounded doubly loud in the silence under the trees. Every inch of this creek was familiar to him. He'd played pirates here as a little kid, with Mum keeping half an eye on him and Loser as she read a magazine on a low branch.

There was the pool he used to fish in, hoping to catch a shark or at least a barramundi, though all it held was tadpoles and dead leaves. There was the old cubby he'd built with Loser when they were in Year Two. Mr Loosley had given them some old corrugated iron and bits of wood and a hammer and nails.

Loser hadn't been so bad back then, thought Mike. Or maybe when you were a little kid you just wanted company. You didn't think what the other person was really like. Or maybe . . . maybe it was a bit of both. Loser was always Loser, but things had changed him too . . .

Mike stopped, out of breath, and leant against a willow tree. He could see his house through the leaves, his bedroom window with the dark blue curtains. He could even see the clock in the kitchen and the dumb kitchen mobile of plastic cups and spoons and forks he'd made as a little kid and Mum refused to take down.

There was Loser's house, too, with its overgrown garden that seemed to cut the house off from the rest of the world, the chook shed leaning slightly to one side, the boat that Mr Loosley had started but never finished

(Loser had said that he was going to sail it round the world), and the two old cars behind the garage for spare parts. He and Loser had pretended to drive them and crash into each other . . .

The Loosley's back fence was too high to get over. He'd have to go through his own garden first, then through the side fence. Luckily, Mum would still be at the gallery . . .

Mike took a deep breath. He looked both ways, then ran across the space between the creek and the fences, through the back gate of his house and up the side of their house. Now all he had to do was . . .

'Mike!'

Mike froze. His mum stared down at him from the kitchen window. She looked older, Mike thought. There were shadows on her face that hadn't been there this morning. 'Mike, darling, what are you . . . what's happened . . . is it all over?'

'Mum, no! Stop!' But it was too late. The face at the window disappeared. Mike heard the back door open and her footsteps clattering down the stairs. 'Mike, I was so worried. I've just been sitting here by the phone. I tried to ring your father but he's not in yet. Tell me . . .'

Mike's heart began to race. What if she stopped him going over to Loser's? What if she called the police to report him for being away from the quarantine area?

What if it *was* a virus? What if he was wrong, and it wasn't poison at all? What if he was infected too, or carried it on his clothes? Mike's heart began to beat hard and painfully. All Mum had to do was come closer and she might be lying on a stretcher too . . .

'Mum, stop!'

She hesitated. 'But, Mike . . .'

'Mum, don't come any closer! Please!'

'I don't understand . . .'

It was no use, thought Mike desperately. Mum still thought of him as a little kid, not to be trusted even to buy a cheese and salad sandwich at lunch time. She'd never listen to him.

Mum stopped in the middle of the kitchen path, next to the lilac tree. 'Mike, what's happened?' she whispered.

'I sneaked out of the hall. There's something I have to do. It's urgent. I can't explain. Just . . . just please, go back in the house and don't tell anyone you saw me.'

Mum shook her head dazedly. Her lipstick was long gone. She looked pale and frightened. She took a step closer. 'Mike . . .'

'No, Mum!' cried Mike. 'Don't you understand? I might be infectious! You have to stay away!'

'Mike, I don't care! You're my son! I just want to . . .'

'Please, Mum! Just for once in my life could you trust me?'

Mum stopped. She stared at him. She was crying, Mike realised, the tears slipping silently down her cheeks. Suddenly she nodded. 'I trust you, Mike,' she said. Her voice was very soft. 'Of course I trust you. Ring me . . . let me know . . .'

'Yes, Mum,' whispered Mike. 'Now go inside. Please. I know what I'm doing. Just go inside.'

Mum hesitated. She looked at him as though she was drinking in his whole appearance, to save it in case she never saw him again. Then she turned and went inside.

CHAPTER 19

FRIDAY, 5.05 P.M.

Mike crept down the path along the side of the house.

On the other side of the fence he could hear the Loosley's chooks, chipping and chupping and pecking at the orange peel and potato peelings in their run. They'd be eyeing the perches, thought Mike, getting ready for he who-gets-the-highest-perch chook discussion before ey went to bed. Far off he could hear the mutter of a set, but it was too faint to tell if it came from the osley's or further up the street.

 all seemed ordinary. If this was a movie, thought e, it wouldn't be like this. There'd be that 'da de da style of really suspenseful music in the round, not the sound of some advertisement for . And the hero wouldn't have crept along a fence among the dog droppings either.

There'd have been . . . what? A car chase probably, with lots of swerves and bangs. Loser would have stolen a car and raced off out of town and Mike would have grabbed one of the SES vehicles . . . Mr Johnstone's old

Mercedes maybe . . . and zoomed off after him. There'd have been speed and screeching tyres and you'd feel like laughing with the excitement of it all . . .

Not like this. Not like this at all. The hero in the movie wouldn't have felt his mind jammed with fear for his friends in hospital, his friends left behind (had anyone else fallen sick while he was away, he wondered).

Fear for himself, too.

Jazz was right, he thought. It didn't matter in movies how many people were killed, as long as the hero and heroine were safe at the end. The killing of bystanders just added to the excitement. But in real life no one was just a bystander. They were people that you knew.

What was Mr Loosley doing, wondered Mike. Was he up with the SES as usual, pretending he knew more than anyone else and telling everyone it wasn't Loser's fault at all? Or was he frantically hunting round the edges of town for his son?

Mike took a deep breath and clambered over the fence between his house and the Loosley's shed. It was an old shed. Mike supposed it had been there when the Loosleys bought the place. If Mr Loosley had built it, one wall would have been only half-finished, or it would still be without a door.

It was a wooden shed, the old yellow paint splintered and showing the dull wood underneath. The small space between the shed and the fence was carpeted with morning glory leaves. Mum always complained when the Loosley's morning glory tendrils poked through the fence. Johnny Shadwell, who came in to do the garden once a fortnight, had to keep cutting it back.

His feet made no sound on the thick mat of vine. Mike stepped carefully round the corner and peered through the dusty window.

The shed was empty. There were only the shelves of bottles and cobwebs and rusty cans filled with second-hand nails, a spade and a mattock at one end and a greasy chainsaw at the other. Mike carefully turned the door handle and stepped inside.

CHAPTER 20

FRIDAY, 5.15 P.M.

'Hello, Mike,' said Loser.

Mike felt his heart expand through his whole body. 'Los . . . Lance!' he corrected. 'Where are you?'

There was a giggle in the dimness. 'Down here,' said Loser.

Mike squinted through the shadow. 'Where? What are you doing down there?'

Loser giggled again from under the dusty shelves and pushed his glasses back up his nose. It was a strange giggle, thought Mike. A little kid's sound, like Loser wanted somehow to be back in the time when they were small and safe.

'No one can find me here,' said Loser seriously, as he huddled under the shelves.

'Well, I just did,' pointed out Mike.

'You're different,' said Loser, still in that strange childlike voice. 'We used to play together, didn't w Mike? Dad said I had to be best friends with you. H said if we were friends your mum would have to giv him a job. Dad said he could look after your place and your mum would pay him because she didn't have anyone else to help her. But I liked you anyway, Mike.'

Mike didn't know how to answer. Maybe there was no answer.

'How many people have died?' asked Loser, in his new small voice.

'I don't know,' said Mike honestly. 'Some are pretty sick.'

'I thought you all would die,' said Loser vaguely, as though he inhabited a different reality to the one where his school companions were dying. 'Hasn't anyone died at all?'

'No,' said Mike. His eyes searched the shelves, one by one. No small bottle there, or there . . . it had been on the second shelf, surely, towards the back . . .

'Oh,' said Loser. He seemed to think for a moment. 'They have to die,' he said seriously. 'If they don't die I won't be on television, will I? Do you think they'll die, Mike?'

Mike didn't answer. That was the shelf! It had to be . . .

'I'm glad you didn't die, Mike,' said Loser matter-of-factly. 'I wanted you to die this morning. But not now. Are you looking for the bottle, Mike?'

'Yes,' said Mike. 'Where is it, Lance?'

Another giggle. 'I've got it here,' said Loser. 'I'm not going to let it go.'

'Is that what you used to poison them with, Lance?' asked Mike quietly.

'You guessed!' said Loser proudly. 'I thought you

might guess. You used to be my friend. You're not dumb like the rest of them. They might do well at school but they're still dumb, that's what Dad says. Dad says I have to show everyone how clever I really am. It was a clever idea, wasn't it?'

'How did you do it?' whispered Mike.

'I bet you can't guess that!' said Loser. 'I'm cleverer than all of you! I said I'd show you and I did! Are the TV cameras out there yet?'

'Lance, please,' cried Mike. 'You've got to tell me what's in that bottle! People are sick! Jazz . . . Jazz's dying . . .'

Loser's eyes were wide and white in the darkness. 'She deserves it,' he whispered.

'Lance . . . she did invite you to her party. Really, she did! Caitlin just didn't give you the envelope. Jazz was really angry when she found out you hadn't got it. She was going to come up and invite you especially at break, but . . . but . . .'

The small huddle that was Loser was silent under the shelves.

'Please!' pleaded Mike. 'Please don't let her die! Tell me what you did!'

Loser said something too low to hear.

'What did you say?' cried Mike. 'Please, Lance!'

'I said I snuck in to the classroom at break and dipped the tops of the pens on the desks in the poison,' whispered Loser. 'I took the top bit of the pens out and dipped them in.'

Mike thought back. There'd been a pen in Mr Simpson's hand as he collapsed. He must have chewed it absent-mindedly. Caitlin had been writing her will. Jazz had written out the instructions from over the phone. He remembered her small white teeth nibbling on the pen. Then she'd made a face and stopped.

'She said there was a funny taste in her mouth . . .' he muttered. So that was how he'd done it. But it still didn't answer the most important question.

'Lance!' he said sharply. 'What's in that bottle?'

'Poison,' whispered Loser.

'What *sort* of poison?'

'I don't know. It killed the dog though. It killed the foxes too. I thought you'd all die quickly like the foxes. You'd all be in class holding your pens and one by one you'd all be dead. Then the TV cameras would come and . . .'

'Lance,' said Mike very carefully. 'Hand me the bottle.'

'No,' said Loser.

'I have to read the label!'

'No,' said Loser. 'You won't give it back to me.'

'Why do you want it back?'

Loser giggled again. But they weren't giggles, Mike realised. They were sobs. 'Dad . . .' he sobbed. 'Everyone . . . I can't go back there, can I? I can't go back to school now. They're going to put me in prison and send me to the electric chair.'

'They won't do that, Lance,' said Mike helplessly. 'We don't have the electric chair in Australia. We don't even kill people here. You're thinking of the movies. This isn't a movie, Lance.'

'I thought, I thought I'd be on TV. I'd be on the news

all over the world,' said Loser. The edge of his glasses gleamed in a stray beam of light. 'I thought people would be afraid of me then. I didn't have a choice! You see that, don't you Mike? I *had* to do it! No one would believe me if I hadn't done it. I had to show them that I was ... I was ... Have they put me on the news yet, Mike?'

'No,' said Mike. He had no idea if anything had been on the news. But he knew with every millimetre of his being that he had to drag Loser back to reality. 'Everyone is upset, that's all.'

'I thought, I thought there'd be lots of cameras and things. They'd all be talking about me and why I'd done it and I could tell them how everyone was mean, how they deserved to die. I thought, I thought Dad would be proud of me if I'm on the news,' said Loser.

Proud that his son is a killer, thought Mike. Even Mr Loosley wasn't as bad as that. But he didn't say anything. 'Please let me see the bottle,' he said instead.

'No,' said Loser. 'I need it now.' All at once Mike realised that the lid was off the bottle.

'No!' he cried.

Loser clung more tightly to the bottle. 'They don't think I'm a hero, do they?' he whispered. 'They just think I'm dumb.'

'Give it to me!' ordered Mike.

Loser lifted the bottle towards his lips. Mike flung himself down, over to Loser, but there was no need. Loser dropped the bottle without drinking. He began to cry.

The bottle rolled over and over on the dirt floor, a small pool of white spilling on the ground. Loser covered his face with his hands as Mike grabbed the bottle.

'I didn't mean to hurt anyone,' gasped Loser between his sobs. 'I didn't mean to do it!'

The words were meaningless. Mike jerked himself back across the damp floor of the shed. He gazed at the label frantically. 'Strychnine,' he whispered.

Loser was suddenly still. He wrapped his arms around himself again. 'What are they going to do to me?' he whispered. 'What will happen now, Mike?'

'I don't know!' Mike fumbled urgently with the phone in his pocket. His fingers almost shook too much to press the numbers. One ring, two rings, three . . . please, please let her answer, he prayed. Please . . . not the answering service . . . please . . .

'Hello?'

'Dr Fallerton, it's Mike, it's strychnine, I think that's how it's pronounced. It wasn't the stuff in the test tube at all. Loser put strychnine on the ends of the pens. Does that help?'

Dr Fallerton's voice choked. 'Yes. Oh, yes, it helps,' she said. 'Mike, I have to go. I have to tell them . . .'

'She's still alive, isn't she?' demanded Mike desperately.

'Yes. Yes. I know what to do now. I'll call back, Mike. I'll call you back.'

The phone went dead.

Lance stared at him, his face white in the dimness of the shed. 'Mike? Mike, will you help me run away? Please, Mike, I can't stay here! I can't!'

Mike dialled again. It was hard to see the numbers. His eyes were blurred, but he wasn't sure if it was sweat or tears.

'Police,' he whispered when they answered. 'Put me onto the police.'

'Please, Mike!'

Mike ignored him. He tried to keep his voice steady as he spoke into the phone. 'Hello? Is that the police? My name is Michael Hammersley. I'm at 15 Waratah Road, Elbow Creek.'

'Mike, you're my friend! You can't tell on me!'

I'm not your friend, thought Mike. I never had the guts to be your friend. But I'm doing the right thing now.

'I'm with Lance Loosley.' His voice sounded like a stranger's, even to him. 'The kid you're looking for. Yeah, the kid with the test tube at the school. But it was poison, not a virus.'

Looser scrabbled over the floor towards him. Mike backed away slowly, cradling the phone. 'Mike, say I didn't mean to do it! Please, Mike!'

'We're around the back in the shed. Please come soon. Please.' He wondered vaguely what else he needed to say, but his mind had gone dead. It was suddenly as though too much had been crammed in it, all through this terrible day.

The mobile phone fell from his fingers. Dimly he could hear a tinny phone voice chattering on the other end, but he ignored it. He leant against the door of the shed, breathing hard, as though he had run a long way.

'Mike?' whispered Loser. He was still inside the shed, away from the light in the doorway. He was shivering, as though the cloak of pretence had fallen away, leaving him in cold reality.

'Yes, Lance,' said Mike.

'Will you stay with me till they come?'

'I'll stay with you,' said Mike. He pushed himself off the door and stepped back into the dimness. He wondered if he should put an arm around Lance's shoulders. But it seemed soppy to do that. So he sat beside him on the cold dirt floor as they listened for the faint sound of the siren in the distance.

CHAPTER 21

SUNDAY, 11.20 A.M.

'It would have made a lousy movie,' whispered Jazz sleepily. Dr Fallerton had warned Mike about the sleepiness. Jazz had been given sedatives to counteract the strychnine. A tube of some clear fluid ran into a needle in her hand. Mike tried not to stare at it. It gave him the creeps.

Silly, he thought, to be nervous of a little needle after all that had happened.

The tiny hospital room's curtains were closed (too much light still hurt Jazz's eyes) but a beam of sunlight shone through the gap between them, lighting up the vases of bright flowers, the giant teddy bear, half the fluffy purple tiger, six squares of the technicolour quilt crocheted by the Gunyabah Senior Citizens, and the massive jar of jelly beans. At least fifty cards, half of them saying 'get well' and the other half 'happy birthday', three new books, two magazines and a plastic box of Mrs Daniel's mushy home-made marshmallow peanut fudge sat in dimness on top of the bedside cupboard.

'Why would it make a lousy movie?' asked Mike softly, just for something to say. Dr Fallerton had warned that he must be very quiet too. Jazz was getting better fast, but any loud noise or movement could still trigger a painful spasm.

'No one died,' whispered Jazz. 'You've got to have lots of bodies in a movie.'

'You're just down on thrillers,' said Mike mildly, though privately he wondered if he'd ever watch one without remembering the past few days. There was nothing thrilling about pain or death when you were close to them. Mike suspected he'd never really feel the same about movies again.

No, there were no bodies. Mr Simpson and Caitlin were recovering too. Spear carriers, thought Mike. Innocent people who got caught up in the story and almost died.

But were they really innocent, he wondered? Caitlin had failed to deliver the invitation. Even Mr Simpson must have known Lance was being picked on, but did nothing.

Who is really innocent, thought Mike. Not me, or Budgie, or Lance's parents or even Mum . . . if we see something is wrong and don't do anything, then maybe we're guilty, too.

Maybe there's no such thing as innocent bystanders, thought Mike, watching Jazz's face on the pillow. The evil emperor's soldiers should help the hero escape, not just stand there doing their jobs. But what should I have done? Not been Lance's friend — you can't force friendship.

But I should have been . . . kind to him. I should have been honest with him, told him what he was doing was dumb instead of laughing behind his back, should have helped him out of the pretend world that his father led him into.

Mike had gone in the police car with Lance, all the way to Gunyabah. But Lance had said nothing after the police arrived. He'd just nodded when they asked him his name. He hadn't looked at Mike as the siren screamed all around them, just huddled in the corner of the seat looking out at the fields as though he never expected to see them again.

Perhaps he wasn't seeing them, thought Mike. Who knows what Lance saw.

The siren screamed, the police officers kept glancing round, as though they expected Lance to try to murder them or Mike, the police wheels pounded on the broken bitumen as though they were chanting deep into Mike's brain:

Which one is guilty,
Which of us three,
Mr Loosley or Loser or me . . .

At Gunyabah police station they'd taken Lance away. Mike had caught a glimpse of Mrs Loosley, her face carved with desperation, frantically running up from the car park, before the police took him to an interview room.

Mr Loosley had still been out searching for Lance with Constable Svenic. With the small part of his mind that could still think at all, Mike was glad that Mr Loosley hadn't arrived at Gunyabah police station yet. He couldn't have faced Mr Loosley.

We are all guilty,
Each of us three,
Mr Loosley and Loser and me . . .

They'd given Mike a cup of tea in the interview room, and one of the constables had gone out and bought him a hamburger, but he couldn't eat it. Mum had arrived, all shaking and with her hair in a mess, and he'd told his story into a tape recorder, and then read it and signed it when the police sergeant typed it out. He'd tried to tell them it wasn't just Lance's fault. It was everyone's fault, but the words wouldn't come.

'You're quite a hero, son,' said the police sergeant, as he finally escorted them out the door.

Mike shook his head. He was no hero. Lance was no villain. Jazz could explain it all to them, he thought vaguely. Jazz would know the words.

'What's going to happen to him?' whispered Jazz from her pillow.

'Lance? I don't know. They say he's sick, mentally sick — that's what the counsellor told us. I don't know if he'll go to prison, or a sort of prison hospital. But I don't think they'll let him go home.' Mike hesitated. 'I don't think he'll want to go home.'

Outside the police station Mum had hugged him for a long time before she'd been able to drive. Dad had been waiting at the house, a look on his face that Mike had never seen before. Things had been . . . different. . . with Dad since then.

'The people from the Department of Health finally turned up,' said Mike. 'Just as it was all over. They wore these respirators and everything Budgie said, but I missed it all.'

Jazz didn't answer. Her eyes were closed, the lashes very black against the milky brown of her face, the pillow a hard white against her hair. She must be asleep again, thought Mike. It was time to go.

He stood up, hesitated, then pressed her hand — the one without the needle. Her fingers closed round his, slowly but firmly. Mike sat down again, his hand still in hers. The sounds of the hospital washed over him: the clink of a trolley in the corridor, a far off beeping, the magpies gurgling outside.

'Mum can't get over how kind everyone's been,' whispered Jazz finally. 'How everyone helped in the emergency. She said she's never seen anything like it. She's talking about staying here. Dad wants to stay too.'

Happiness began to soak through Mike, warm as the sunlight. But he just said, 'That's good.'

'Shouldn't be too hard,' said Jazz sleepily. 'Not with the shortage of doctors out here. Mike?'

'Mmmm?'

'Will you take me fishing when I get out of here? To that place on the farm you told me about? Mum says I'll be out in a few days.'

'Sure,' said Mike. He supposed he'd be spending lots more time out at the farm with Dad now, anyway.

Suddenly it was extraordinarily good to be alive. Everything looked clearer, brighter, than he had ever seen it. Even the old pepper tree through the crack in the curtains seemed dipped in gold. Was that what happened when you faced death, Mike wondered. Suddenly you saw life as well?

He smiled, and let the sunlight seep through him as he sat there, holding Jazz's hand.

Hitler's Daughter
Jackie French

Anna's story about Hitler's daughter haunts
Mark. Could it have been true? Did Hitler's
daughter really exist? If Mark had a father like
Hitler, could he love him?

'A story that will fascinate and involve all
thoughtful young readers; it is a true original,
beautifully told and impossible to put down.'
Wendy Cooling

'An outstanding novel told through the power of
a compelling storyteller.' *Reading Time*

The Children's Book Council of Australia's
Book of the Year 2001

Winner of a National Literacy Association's
WOW! Award 2002

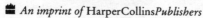
An imprint of HarperCollins*Publishers*